LANDQUAKER

BOOKS BY DEAN F. WILSON

THE CHILDREN OF TELM

Book One: The Call of Agon
Book Two: The Road to Rebirth
Book Three: The Chains of War

THE GREAT IRON WAR

Hopebreaker
Lifemaker
Skyshaker
Landquaker
Worldwaker

THE GREAT IRON WAR - BOOK FOUR

LANDQUAKER

DEAN F. WILSON

Cover illustration by Duy Phan

First Edition 2016

ISBN 978-1-909356-14-6

DIOSCURI PRESS

Published by Dioscuri Press
Dublin, Ireland

www.dioscuripress.com
enquiries@dioscuripress.com

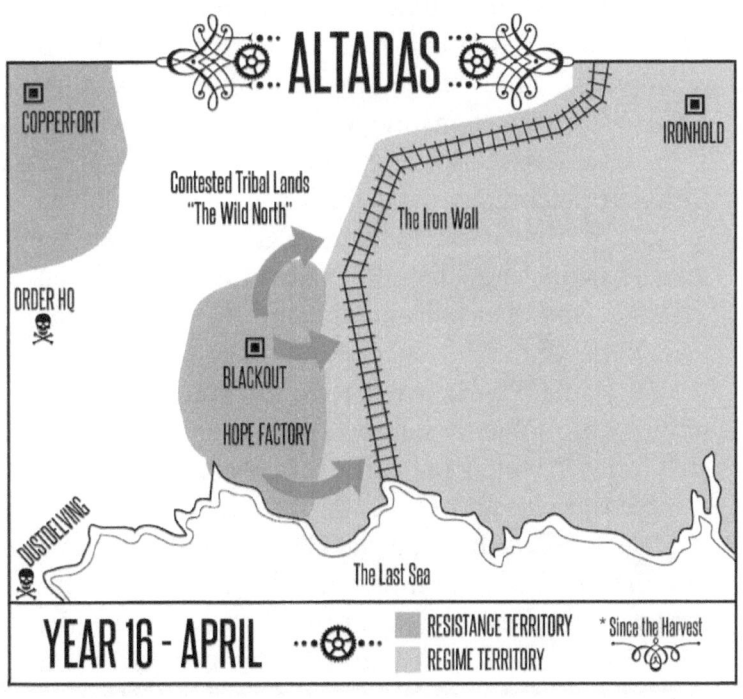

ALTADAS

COPPERFORT

IRONHOLD

Contested Tribal Lands
"The Wild North"

The Iron Wall

ORDER HQ

BLACKOUT

HOPE FACTORY

DUSTDELVING

The Last Sea

YEAR 16 - APRIL

RESISTANCE TERRITORY
REGIME TERRITORY

* Since the Harvest

THE GREAT IRON WAR

In the world of Altadas, in the year 1888 of the Second Era, women everywhere dreamed of a coming desert. Those who were already pregnant miscarried, and those who became pregnant did not give birth to human children. An invasion had begun.

The newborns had no horns or marks, and so they were loved and reared like all the others. It would take time before anyone realised what they really were, before anyone would call them demons.

These events were marked by the arrival of strangers claiming to be from a distant land. The people of Altadas called them Pilgrims, but they did not know just how far they had come, nor by what strange doors they had entered, nor exactly what they had come for.

The first Pilgrims were scouts, but subsequent waves were soldiers, sent by a man who would later call himself the Iron Emperor. He promised his people iron. He gave them war instead.

They called that year the Harvest, and it became the first year of a new, darker calendar. Sand swept through the great chasms in the sky from where the demons came, the dust of a world that they had dried up. Ahead of the landships went great sandstorms, until the green grasses became an endless red desert.

In Altadas, steam powers industry, but iron powers war. The abundant metal, idolised by the invaders, and depleted in their home world, became a beacon to the demons, and was the foundation upon which they would build their new civilisation. They called themselves the Iron Empire. Their enemies simply called them the Regime.

As war began in the east, few among the Resistance knew that their own children were not really theirs. The invaders had mastered a magical technique to control the birth channels of a people they desired to conquer. Thus with one hand they would wield might, and with the other they would use guile, infiltrating and eradicating their enemies, anyone who would dare defy the Iron Emperor, who had brought his people to this promised land.

Yet iron is more to the demons than just a metal. When broken down into its basic elements, it provides the key ingredient of the necessary sustenance of the invaders. To some it is a drug. To them, symbolising everything they were promised, and everything they were leaving behind, it is Hope.

As one civilisation crumbled, and a new empire was founded on its remains, there were some who refused to live out their last days under the iron grip of their new ruler. They made a promise of their own: to fight, with everything they had, for the fate of humanity.

Thus began the Great Iron War.

CONTENTS

1	A Shroud on the City	11
2	The Long Spyglass	20
3	The Battle Map	26
4	The Negotiaton Team	33
5	The Wild North	40
6	Silver in the Sand	53
7	Wagon War	62
8	Totem	70
9	Surrounded	75
10	The Dust Riders	84
11	The Last of the Green Grass	88
12	The Council of the Land	95
13	War Dance	104
14	One Too Many Chieftains	108
15	Part of the Tribe	116
16	The Gathering	121
17	The Crocodile	125
18	The Iron Medicine	130
19	Project Trident	141
20	The Central Prong	148
21	The Masquerade March	153
22	The Old Trench Tunnels	162
23	Magician Down	169
24	Double Deception	172
25	Changing Weapons	181
26	On the Edge	186
27	All Aboard	191
28	Tracking Traitors	200
29	The Conductor	205

Chapter

30	Ghost Train	210
31	Stampede of the Oxen	213
32	Quake	219
33	Alma Mater	225
34	The Controller	233
35	Rain on the Rails	237
36	The Carriage Smog	243
37	Awakening	250

Chapter One

A SHROUD ON THE CITY

The citizens of Blackout scrubbed the city clean, until they revealed beneath its recent coat of red, the greys and blacks that previously lived there. Half the population had perished in the battles, and the other half were perishing from a shortage of food, and a shortage of will to keep on fighting, or keep on living.

Rommond appointed several of his lieutenants to train some of the more supportive members of the city's militia to police the streets, and when that failed, he roamed the dimly-lit back-alleys himself, and this soon put a stop to the looting and the rioting. Yet with plans in the works to take down the Iron Wall, the general knew that he could not keep an iron grip on the old capital while trying to reach with the other hand to the enemy's neck.

"We risk losing our foothold here," he confided in Brooklyn, as he often did in years past. It was a strange thing to be able to do again, and it was simultaneously comforting and unsettling. Brooklyn was not a strategist, but he was a good listener. While Rommond was full of the aphorisms of battle, Brooklyn had those of his people to fall back upon.

"If you do not move forward as the world moves forward, then you do not just stay still—you move back."

"Yes," Rommond said with a sigh. "We have to press our advantage. They'll expect us to wait. That's what we did before. Build up our defences. We tried that, and it didn't work. We can't afford to let them mount a counter-attack. I feel this game of war is coming to an end, and I have to go all in."

Taberah had participated in the battle, but she did not participate in the battle's aftermath. She became a hermit, hiding away in a room of The Olive Inn, Jacob's old haunt. What haunted her was something different, something that travelled with her. Rommond paid the landlord handsomely to turn the inn into a base for the Regime, but Jacob wondered if maybe he was just buying Taberah a refuge, a space to grieve.

The landlord Gus spotted Jacob loitering outside, buffing the brickwork with his back. "You still owe me for your room," he grunted.

"I thought the general paid for it," Jacob said.

"Ha! He paid for its current use, not its past. I wasn't born yesterday, you know."

"Good," Jacob said. "Guess that makes you human then."

He hurried off, leaving the landlord to dwell on that quip. Banter came easier than coils. If only it could pay the rent. *Maybe it's not so bad with Rommond's lot*, Jacob pondered. *At least he's a landlord who doesn't charge*. It did not take long to consider the real payment, the one that so many paid: life.

* * *

Jacob wanted to visit Taberah many times, but there was always something, or someone, to get in the way. On most occasions it was Doctor Mudro, who became an almost permanent warden of the building, appearing around corners as if from a puff of smoke. Still he puffed on the smoke of the weed, from which he seemed to avail of an equally permanent supply.

"Going somewhere?" Mudro asked on this latest occasion, when Jacob was almost certain no-one was around.

"Hell, Mudro!" Jacob exclaimed. "You'll give someone a heart attack if you keep … *manifesting* like that."

Mudro chuckled. "I've got to keep up the act."

"What act?"

"I don't know," the doctor said, with an overly-dramatic wave of his hand. "I guess it helps to think of all this, this world, as a kind of stage. Seems like we have more control then." He looked away wistfully, as if he saw a story unfolding in the smoke. "What if it was all just some giant magic show?"

"If it is," Jacob said, "we might be heading for the big finale."

"A show-stopper, that."

Jacob smirked. "But what about an encore?"

"It depends who's left to do it."

The smuggler nodded solemnly. "So, what are you doing here anyway? Shouldn't you be helping sew people up?"

Mudro scowled. "I've been banished."

Jacob raised an eyebrow. "Banished? You're getting more metaphysical by the day."

"Not from some magic circle," the doctor protested. "From the infirmary."

"Let me guess … Lorelai?"

Mudro grumbled at the name. "She seems to have a pretty good *handle* on things."

"Yeah, but she's only one person."

Person, Jacob thought to himself. *Does that count for demons too*?

"So am I," the doctor said, and he seemed hurt. "But I'm one person who might 'sew your arm on in the wrong place.'"

"Did she say that?"

"Not in so many words."

"You did some magic to read her mind?"

Mudro rolled his eyes.

"So you're out of a job," Jacob said. "Is this why you're taking up door duty?"

Mudro feigned surprise. "I haven't the slightest idea what you mean."

Jacob simpered.

"Besides," Mudro said, "what are *you* doing here?"

"Looking for a job. Know any takers?"

Mudro did not smile, and the mood soured instantly. He leant in close, close enough to smell the leaf on his breath. "You should leave her alone for a bit."

"I just wanted to make sure she's okay."

"She's not. You know that without seeing her."

Jacob hung his head. "Yeah, but maybe the company will help."

"I don't think so, Jacob. Seeing the baby's father will just remind her of the baby."

Jacob sighed. "I hadn't thought of it like that."

"How are *you* doing anyway?" Mudro prodded Jacob's shoulder with his pipe. "This doesn't just affect her."

"I'm okay, I guess," Jacob replied. "I'd kind of gotten used to the idea of a little tyke." He swallowed hard; it was harder for his mind to swallow the thought of it. "Even started thinking of a couple of names."

Mudro pursed his lips. "She wouldn't let you pick the name. That, I can promise you."

"I don't know. I think I probably could have persuaded her."

"No," the doctor stated. "It was going to be Elizah or it wasn't going to be anything at all."

The thought was disquieting. It left Jacob with many difficult questions in his mind. *What if it was a boy? What if it was not what Taberah wanted?* He dared not dwell enough on them to find the answers.

Jacob followed Mudro's advice for several more days, but he felt compelled to see Taberah, to be there for her. He thought solitude could not be good for her. He knew that, though he once thought otherwise, it was not good for him. He found a way into the inn late at night when Mudro was not around, though even then he expected to find the doctor shuffling cards in every corner. He knocked on the door to Taberah's room, which was located in one of the more dimly-lit corridors, but there was no answer.

He jiggled the handle, and the door creaked

open. It was the kind of creak that made him think of a haunted house, but the dying flames in the oil lamps did not help. He thought maybe it was a good sign that she had not locked the door, but then again Mudro was his own kind of latch. Jacob stepped in slowly, his shadow squeezing in behind him. He was almost too quiet, because she did not seem to notice him. She sat on the edge of her bed, hunched over her diary. She did not write in it. She just stared at the blank pages.

"I came to talk," Jacob said.

She looked up at him blankly, then returned her gaze to those empty pages. Her eyes seemed empty too. Who knew what, if anything, filled her heart.

Jacob bit his lip. He could not think of what to say.

"I ... I came to talk," he tried again, approaching her bed.

She set her icy eyes on him once more. "Do you know why I keep a diary?"

Jacob shook his head. Body language was a little easier.

"I keep it to remind me of who I am," she said, clutching it tightly, digging her nails into the leather. She waved it at him, like a cry for help, so he crouched down beside her. "I keep it to stop me from getting lost."

She looked back at the blank pages. If it reminded her of who she was, it reminded her of nothing, of emptiness. If she could not find the words to write, she could not find herself in the vacancies between the faint lines of the pages.

"Maybe you don't need that to know who you

are," Jacob suggested. He thought it might sound trite. He was better at jokes than words of wisdom.

"You don't know me, Jacob. You think you do." She gestured to herself. "*I* don't know me. I don't know who I am." Her lip trembled. "I feel like I'm losing myself again. I feel like I'm being washed away."

Jacob took her hand. He was surprised that she did not resist. The fight in her was gone.

"Maybe you need an anchor," he said.

"Maybe I just need to let go," she replied.

"No," Jacob insisted, and he squeezed her hand tighter. "You have to keep fighting."

"I don't want to fight any more," she said. "I've been fighting all my life. Why does everything have to be a struggle? Why can't it be easy just this once?"

"It wouldn't be worth it if it was easy."

"It doesn't seem worth it even when it's hard."

Jacob did not know what to say. Just when he was trying to formulate some words of reassurance, something changed in Taberah. He started to see why she did not know who she was any more, because for the briefest of moments he did not recognise her. Even her shadow shifted.

"*They* stole her from me," she hissed. "And just when I was getting her back, they stole her again." She slammed her journal down on the floor beside her, where it made a thunderous thud.

The moment passed, and she broke down, the tears tumbling from her eyes like her ruby hair tumbled down her shoulders, water to temper fire. But the tears did not douse the flames; they were like tears of oil, igniting the tempest even more.

17

"The doctor said—"

"I don't care what he said," she interjected, lashing him with her eyes, as if he had stolen her child. He looked to the ground, and he was surprised to discover that he felt shame. *I didn't do enough*, he thought. But what more could he have done? *Maybe I could have saved her.*

Taberah reached down to the crumpled diary. The pages were still empty, but now a few of them were torn. How many of those diaries she had filled up in years past, Jacob did not know. He only knew that when that little heartbeat stopped, the ink no longer flowed.

She held that diary in her hands, and it must have meant more to her than Jacob knew. In it, she might have documented her struggle. In it, she likely recorded her sorrow. She looked at the leather cover as if she could see something in the grain. Perhaps she saw a memory.

Her eyes were red, and her lip quivered once more. He had never seen her like this—so vulnerable. What fire there was, it was still there, but it was a tiny thing, like the tiny hand she might have then been holding.

Jacob took her in his arms. She struggled at first, but her strikes were weak, and her touch was unrecognisable. In time, as he continued to hold her close, she no longer fought him. The anger left her, and there was only grief. But it was enough to consume her, and to consume any in the room. He tried to hold back his own tears. He had to be strong for her. He did not get to cry for that child he would not have. She cried for the both of them.

Her wails were piercing. They sounded deathly. They sounded ghostly. Her own Iron Wall crumbled, and there was a violent sea behind, a sea where even sorrows drowned, where even pain gave out its own death cry. That night, few in the inn slept soundly. Many did not believe in ghosts, but when they heard Taberah's woeful howls, they shivered, and thought they saw something different in the shadows of their rooms.

Chapter Two

THE LONG SPYGLASS

Rommond found Brooklyn as he often had in years past, tending to equipment as if it were an animal, a wild horse brought into civilisation, yet never fully tamed. Brooklyn sat cross-legged in a circle of parts, like one of the meditation circles of his people, and he polished several cogs before laying them down in order of size. Rommond smiled as he watched, taking care not to disturb him, and taking pride in knowing that the ordering by size was something he took up from Rommond—he was gifted, but he used to be messy.

"I know you are there," Brooklyn said.

"I know you know," Rommond replied, his smile widening.

"Join me."

Rommond sat down beside Brooklyn, grunting as his tired limbs clicked into place. He was getting old. Somehow Brooklyn looked the same. Their parting had not aged him as much as it had the general. Maybe it was the machine in him, immune to the mechanics of time.

"I see you smile," Brooklyn commented, "but your smile is different."

Rommond could not help but think that, in Brooklyn's case, the difference was that he no longer seemed to smile.

"The tooth, you mean?" the general replied. He felt suddenly a little self-conscious, as if a part of his uniform was out of place.

"Yes. What happened to it?"

"Let's just say a debt had to be paid."

"The Treasury?"

"Yes," Rommond said with a grin, wide enough to show the glimmer. "I guess it's fitting that the replacement is gold."

Brooklyn forced the tiniest of smiles, which looked even tinier on his small mouth. That he had to force anything was worrying. It used to be that things came naturally to him.

"What are you making?" Rommond asked. He did not touch anything. He knew well that he did not fully understand how Brooklyn operated, but knew with greater certainty that nothing was arbitrary. Everything was a kind of ritual.

Brooklyn held up a tiny lens. The light caught it, shining beams upon the many parts attached to it. There were adjustable mirrors, moved by minute cogs, and several other glass pieces, concave and convex, arranged into a little box.

"An eyepiece?" Rommond quizzed.

"For big eye."

Rommond raised an eyebrow. "It's a small piece."

"Of bigger glass." Brooklyn gestured towards the spyglass perched upon the city's wall, aimed at the Landquaker, just like the barrel of that scope was aimed at the city, with ammunition in place of an eye.

"Will this help us see better?"

"See farther than any glass can see," Brooklyn said, but he sunk his head, "if I can get it all to work."

"If anyone can do it," Rommond said, "you can."

Brooklyn did not seem so confident, and this worried Rommond. When the fabled mechanic took on a new project, it was from inspiration, and the fires never burned out. Even when he was finished, those fires would simply transmute into the enthusiasm for another creation, another invention. He said the spirits led him, and Rommond thought that if they really were spirits, they led him well. But why did it seem like they did not lead him now?

Brooklyn worked tirelessly on the spyglass throughout the night, shunning sleep. He used to work until his dreams pulled him into slumber, and then woke periodically with new vigour, new ideas, and new guidance from the machine spirits. But now the dreams did not tug him, and the night was spent in restless toil, trying to get the material cogs to work, when the mental ones would not. Rommond also did not sleep that night, and he would have liked to have thought he turned his back on slumber in sympathy with Brooklyn, but instead his mind was restless with worry.

When the cogs of night turned and produced the gentle glow of day, Rommond found an exhausted Brooklyn putting the finishing touches on the enhanced spyglass. His clothes were covered in oil, and his hands in soot.

"All done?" the general asked.

Brooklyn stifled a grumble. He was not one to complain.

"Can I look?"

"You can look, but can you see?" Brooklyn asked in turn, the frustration etched into the dark circles around his eyes, the soot of sleep.

Rommond peered into the spyglass, and bit his lip. It was all a blur.

"It's … a little foggy."

Brooklyn took a deep breath, letting it out very slowly so that it would not sound like a sigh.

"Maybe it just needs a quick adjustment," Rommond suggested. *It shouldn't*, he thought. *Nothing of Brooklyn's ever did before.*

Brooklyn tinkered with the knobs and nozzles, punctuating the clicks and clangs with a bang from his spanner. Rommond was not a mechanic, but he thought that was less a technique of repair and more an expression of frustration. It was awkward to stand there, and difficult to watch Brooklyn struggle with what at one time came with ease. The general wondered if he should perhaps walk away, give his partner some room to breathe, and time to calm down, but he stayed through the anguish and the toil, periodically glancing into the glass, until Brooklyn turned the nozzle again, and the sight sharpened.

"Wait," Rommond said. "I see something now."

Then he saw it: the Landquaker in all its might and beauty, that intimidating barrel on that intimidating frame. It had a giant red hull, beneath which were two long carriages, each on a set of eight wheels, four per side, connected together with rods. The train could bend ever so slightly in the centre, just enough to get it around the corners of the tracks, but otherwise it was designed to chug along in a single, devastating line. On either end, its ornate panels and designs were still visible, though these were somewhat faded from the time when the Resistance owned that vehicle. On the chassis were the emblems of the Regime, which were not faded at all. From the roof protruded the colossal barrel of the gun, which could fire 400mm shells. When fired, the main body of the train slid back, and the space between the two carriages was specifically designed for this recoil. Its shots were best fired from a stable position, but the design also allowed for it to fire when moving. The sliding recoil would slow its advance, but it would not stop it entirely. Nothing could stop the Landquaker. That is why it became the Gate in the Iron Wall.

Rommond withdrew from the spyglass, happy to be able to see, but unhappy at the sight of someone else in the distance playing with one of his favourite toys. He wanted it back, and back in one piece, but just like the jealousy of a child, if he could not get it back intact, then he would destroy it.

"Well," the general said. "I can see it perfectly. Almost too perfectly." He gently patted the barrel of the scope. "Now that you've worked your wonders on this beauty, it'll need a name. How about the Long Spyglass?"

Brooklyn's eyes welled up, and Rommond grabbed his hand.

"What's wrong?" he asked. "You got it working."

"It is not that," Brooklyn said, turning away.

"What is it then?" Rommond asked. "Do you not forgive me?"

Brooklyn turned back, surprised. "There is nothing to forgive."

"Then why are you turning away from me?"

The glisten in Brooklyn's eyes was his only answer.

"What are you afraid of?" Rommond asked, gripping Brooklyn's hand tighter, trying to tell him in that grip that there was no need to be afraid.

"They did something to me," Brooklyn revealed. "The Regime. They changed me."

"But that's over now. You're free."

Brooklyn shook his head. "But I'm not. They're still there somewhere. I can *feel* them. I can feel them like I used to feel the spirits."

"You mean you don't feel the spirits any more?"

Brooklyn raised his mechanical arm. "Not since *this*. I can still hear them, from a distance, but only their anger, their frustration, their fear. I hear them speaking, but they no longer speak to me. But the Regime. They have taken their place."

"But we removed most of the implants," Rommond said.

Brooklyn sighed. "Most."

"Then what are you afraid of?"

Brooklyn trembled. "I am afraid I am going to betray you."

Chapter Three

THE BATTLE MAP

Beneath the central plaza of Blackout, where Lorelai continued her endless labour on the people's many wounds, there was a converted cellar, a bunker even, with reinforced walls to withstand a bomb or earthquake—though maybe not the shells of the Landquaker. The sewers there were converted into passages, leading to all manner of locations across the city, including a small hatch in The Olive Inn. The general revealed that this was an addition made by the ever-resourceful Treasury. Jacob was amused to discover this, considering how handy it would have been as a smuggling route.

That bunker became the War Room, and many of the leading faces of the Resistance gathered there to discuss the next push. The plans for attacking the Landquaker were well under way, but the more tiny markers that were placed on the map, the larger the model of the Landquaker looked in comparison. It was a crude model, devoid of the elaborate markings that Brooklyn liked to finish his machines with, like swirling tattoos for a tribe made of metal—but the crudeness highlighted just how devastating that railway gun really was.

"We'll need decoys," Rommond said, looking to Doctor Mudro, whose intensely furrowed brow was visible through the smoke.

"We'll need a lot of them," Mudro replied.

"I think we might need more than decoys," Jacob said. "Hell, we could do with a whole magic show." He turned to the doctor, who was absent-mindedly poking around in the pocket of his waistcoat, as if the decoys were in there. "I hope you've got more than rabbits up your sleeve."

"I think we'll leave magic out of this," Rommond said.

Taberah glanced at Mudro, and he looked back. It was a fleeting look, but Jacob felt like maybe it was something more.

"If you give me enough hands, I can build several platoons of fake landships here," Mudro said, pointing his pipe to a strip of land south of the nearest Hope factory. "This should make it look like we're amassing our forces for an attack at the southern end of the Iron Wall. The Regime will likely amass its own landships there in response."

"What about the Hope factory?" Jacob asked. "Is that still under Regime control?"

"No," Rommond said. "We sent a scouting party there yesterday, and it's been deserted. We have them in retreat for now, which is why we cannot delay too long if we want to press our advantage."

"And you think they'll really fall for those decoys?" Jacob wondered.

"They'll be made of wood," Mudro said, "but they'll look very real, especially from afar. We'll have a tough time disguising our real forces, and a tougher time again getting them anywhere near the Landquaker."

"Don't you worry about that," Rommond said. "If you draw their eye one way, I'll poke out the other."

"I'll do my sleight of hand," Mudro said, with a wave of his own, "but I need more hands to get those decoys made in time."

"You'll get them," the general replied, nodding to Alakovi. "I think we'll need all your Vixens working on this, Ana. We really need these decoys done and dusted within the next few days. A week tops."

"What can I do?" Whistler asked. Though this was supposed to have been a meeting of a select few, he had begged Jacob to sneak him in. Jacob could not resist using the new smuggling route for something. Taberah rolled her eyes at the pair of them.

Rommond frowned. "Perhaps you'll attend meetings to which you were not invited."

Whistler pouted. "But I can help."

"We'll find something for you," the general said, before turning back to the battle map.

"So we'll have decoys," Jacob said, "but what about the real thing?"

Rommond sighed. "We're working on some new landships, but we'll be lucky to have a single platoon ready in time."

"Do we have no allies?"

"No."

"Maybe we find some," Brooklyn suggested.

Everyone turned to him, Rommond most of all. Brooklyn looked awkward and very self-conscious in the spotlight. He was soft-spoken and had to avail of a lull in the conversation before he would interject.

"My people will not fight war," he said, "but there are many tribes who fight Regime for years in disputed lands. They fight even Landquaker, though alone they do not win. But together, with us ... maybe."

"I tried to get the tribes' support before," Rommond said. "Several times. It didn't do any good."

"We got Brooklyn out of it," Taberah said. She did not seem as broken now. For the good of the Resistance, she put on a show of strength. "If we got one more like him, that'd probably be enough."

"Things have changed," Brooklyn said. "Their views may have changed too."

"It's worth a shot," Jacob added. "Otherwise, we don't really have an army at all."

When the meeting ended, they all turned to leave, but Rommond gestured to Alakovi. "Stay back a moment." There was nothing in his voice that betrayed his intent, but his eyes were severe. Jacob was tempted to smile at the Copper Matron as he passed, but he thought better of it. It did not seem like she would be smiling when she eventually got to leave the bunker.

"What is it, sir?" she asked when the room had cleared. Mudro's smoke lingered.

"You're awfully polite today," Rommond replied. "Pity you weren't so polite when I wasn't around."

Alakovi did not respond, but she scrunched her mouth, as if she was crushing someone between her teeth. Rommond knew well who that someone was.

"Sit down," the general said.

"I'm more a standin' type o' woman."

Rommond glared at her. "No 'sir', this time?" he asked. "Sit down," he added, sterner than before. While everyone who knew him was aware that he had a habit of laying down his gun to finish a conversation, he had a way of doing the same with his voice.

She sat. Anyone who knew *her* would have been surprised to see it. She towered over Rommond, in height and width, and her multicoloured mohawk rose further still, but now that she was seated, he towered over her, and he cast a tall and intimidating shadow, perfectly exemplifying the contours of his uniform.

"I know what happened up there," he said, pointing to the ceiling. "In the skies, when I handed the airship over to Taberah."

"You don't know the whole of it," Alakovi responded.

"I know enough."

"I was tryin' to protect you, Rommond."

"I don't need protecting," he stated. "I need people I can trust."

"And you *can* trust me," Alakovi replied. "You can't trust *her*!"

"Taberah might skirt the edges, but she is one of us." He paced around the room, his shadow pacing with him. "But *you*," he said, drawing out the word. "What you did is not our way. What you did was … it was demonic."

"I'm no demon!" she cried.

"And yet you acted like one."

She bashed her fist on her thigh. "I didn't come here to be interrogated."

"I didn't come to Blackout to have my best betray me."

"I didn't betray you," she pleaded. "Don't you see?" She pointed her pudgy finger to an empty space to her left, where Taberah previously stood. "She's the betrayer. Don't think she's let up wantin' your position. Soon as you go down, she'll be clamberin' over your body to get in your chair. Mark my words, Rommond. And I'll bet she's the one who guns you down too."

"Enough!" Rommond shouted, banging his own fists on the table. It was rare to see him angry, and rarer to seem him violent outside battle. He shook his head and sighed. "What am I going to do with you?"

She looked away. "I care about you, Rommond. I care like a mother cares. I'm not just the Matron of the Copper Vixens, you know. Who else is going to look out for you?"

"You have a funny way of showing it, Ana."

"I never said I was perfect."

"I never thought you'd be a problem."

She folded her arms, and her muscles bulged. "She's the problem, Rommond. You're too close to her to see."

"And *you* can see how close we are," Rommond said. "And you still tried to hurt her. And so you hurt me."

"I meant to protect you."

"Well, we all know the saying about good intentions. What I need are good actions."

"What do you want me to do?"

"I want you to do your job, and no more. You can be the Copper Matron, but don't be a matron to me. I'm not your son, Ana, and the way you acted up there on the Skyshaker, I wouldn't have you as a mother."

Her heavy breathing continued, but she looked less intense than before.

"If you lay a finger on Taberah again," the general continued, "there will be no place for you here, no seat for you to refuse to sit on. You go do your job, and earn back the respect you squandered in the skies."

She opened her mouth to speak, but he placed his pistol on the table and turned away. He heard the creaking of the chair as she struggled up, and her downtrodden steps as she sauntered away. He also thought he heard her whimper, and hoped the copper would not corrode from the tears.

Chapter Four

THE NEGOTIATION TEAM

The Skyshaker loomed over the city, with long ropes hauling the shell of the Hopebreaker to Blackout's worker district. Rommond followed on the ground, and others trailed behind him. To any onlookers it almost seemed like a funeral procession. When they arrived, the carcass of the Hopebreaker was set down, and Rommond placed the nameplate beside it.

Brooklyn drew up close, and the general linked his arm.

"Can you fix it?" Rommond asked.

Brooklyn did not stir. "The spirits can fix anything," he said. "But me?"

"Can they fix a broken heart?" Rommond kept his eyes set on the ruin of the landship before him, as if it were the burned metal shell that had for so long encased his heart. "Only you can fix that for me."

Brooklyn was silent for a time. "What will you take north? Are any landships ready?"

"They're all in pretty bad shape," Rommond said. "We could take the Skyshaker."

"If we wanted to be shot down."

"It's a fast ship."

"My people have fast dart and fast arrow," Brooklyn said, looking up at the airship hovering gloriously above the city, its many wounds patched up, as if it were the general's heart now. "And fast desire to shoot down what should not fly."

"It's a great pity they're not all like you," Rommond replied.

Brooklyn raised his mechanical hand. He did not respond, but the gesture said enough.

"I'd rather not bring an army into tribal land," the general said, directing Brooklyn's attention elsewhere. "Maybe we should use a transport vehicle like the Silver Ghost."

"That is wise. Better to be ambassador."

"Perhaps, but I tend to negotiate with my gun."

"Better to bring other ambassador then."

"I'm not sure who can convince the tribes to join our cause. We weren't that successful on that front before. I have my doubts."

"Many things have changed," Brooklyn said softly. "Who convinced city's people to fight?"

Rommond paused for a moment. "I think it was Jacob."

"Then maybe your doubts have you."

Rommond smiled slightly. "Maybe I *could* do with a little more belief," he said. *But Jacob?* he thought. *If he cracks jokes with the Udanudaga, they might crack his skull open.* He almost heard the smuggler's retort in his head: *It'd be one hell of a negotiation.*

Jacob was surprised to receive a summons from the general, delivered by two of Rommond's smartly-dress lieutenants. When he arrived, he surveyed the general's selection for the mission. There really was not many of them: Rommond, Brooklyn, Taberah, and Jacob. While he had plenty of experience working on his own, he had learned quickly with the Resistance that having a few extra bodies helped when the bodies started piling up. With such small numbers, he felt increasingly like he might be one of them.

"This is a skeleton crew," Rommond declared, rapping his knuckles on the hull of the Silver Ghost, whose exterior lanterns were the only light illuminating the negotiation team.

"Is that your way of saying we're already dead?" Jacob asked with a smirk.

The general grumbled. "We're not going to have much in the way of firepower, so we need to keep a low profile, and stay out of any of the conflicts between the various tribes. We're there to get them involved in our war, not to get involved in theirs."

Jacob raised his hand. "Wouldn't it make more sense to solve their differences so they can all side with us?"

Rommond forced a smile. "Good luck with that."

"I want to come," Whistler said, emerging from the shadows. Jacob had taught him well—perhaps too well.

Rommond shook his head. "You again," he said. "It's just as well you're on our side with all this sneaking around."

"What other side would I be on?" the boy asked. Jacob knew that he wondered if this was a slight against the demon side of him.

"I didn't mean it like that," the general said, rolling his eyes.

"So, can I come?"

"It's too dangerous for you."

Whistler looked to the ground. "You said you'd find something for me."

"Something else. There's lots that needs doing in the city."

"It's not safe," Taberah said, reaching her hand towards Whistler's shoulder, but he recoiled. He bumped into Jacob, and the smuggler instinctively put his hand on the boy's other shoulder, and he did not retreat from that.

"It's not safe here either," Jacob replied. "It's not safe anywhere. Let him come if he wants to. He's old enough to make these choices. Hell, if there's one thing I've learned here in Altadas, it's that the sand and the sun doesn't discriminate."

"I'm trying to protect the boy from danger," Rommond said. "You're just trying to protect him from disappointment."

Jacob scoffed. "Just because we don't have many children left, doesn't mean we have to lock them all up for safekeeping." He could not help but think of his days in the workhouse, and could not help but hear the sound of the lock.

Brooklyn whispered something to Rommond, and the general sighed. Whistler's eyes brightened. "He can come," Rommond said, "but on one—"

"He's not coming," Taberah interjected, placing her hands on her hips.

Whistler's head sunk again.

"This is *my* sortie," the general said.

The fire was back in her, even though the wax was low. "This is *my* son."

Jacob was tempted to say: *So now you choose to be a mother*, but he knew it was unfair of him. She did not get to choose when Domas held her down. And she did not get to choose when she lost Elizah, the first or the second time.

Rommond looked at Brooklyn, who gave the slightest of shrugs. They might have been ambassadors, but it did not seem like either of them could negotiate with Taberah on this issue.

"I'm not a kid any more," Whistler protested. "I should be able to do what I want."

"Those are the words of every child," Taberah replied.

Later that day, Rommond summoned Brooklyn to his quarters in The Olive Inn. Despite all the work he had to do to prepare for the coming battles, everything in his room was neatly arranged. There were a lot of things there, salvaged from the Lifemaker and Skyshaker, including a small mechanical bird in a cage.

"I remember making this," Brooklyn said. "Does it still fly?"

"Wind it up and find out."

Brooklyn took it out of the cage gently, as if it were a real bird. He wound the spring, and it fluttered around the room, before returning to his finger. "I can send this out with message to my people, to call

Land Council."

"Wonderful!" Rommond declared.

Brooklyn put the bird back and wandered around the room.

"You kept this?" he asked, running his fingers over the nameplate from which he drew his name. It had a prominent position behind Rommond's desk.

The general smiled. "Of course."

"I thought maybe, when you thought ..."

"No. That only made me want to keep it even more."

"I remember working on that landship," Brooklyn said. "That seems so long ago now … when I chose who I am. No more Kia-ooba-lukassa then. But … am I still Brooklyn now?"

"Maybe this will make you feel more yourself," Rommond said, holding up a multicoloured blanket, upon which were many buttons of all shapes and sizes, and here and there a cog or two.

Brooklyn was visibly surprised. It was a relic of his past, a talisman of his people. He held the blanket up. Every string and thread had a purpose, a different colour, a different path. They represented the many tribes that lived in what his people called the Uga Ludomu, the Forgotten Lands. For generations they were ignored by the "civilised" people who lived to the east, south, and west. Even the demons struggled to take territory there, but what they could not take, they destroyed, and so they scoured the land—and while the demons might have forgotten about those days, the land remembered.

"So much history," Brooklyn whispered.

"Your history," Rommond said. "Now you can sew on some more buttons."

"What about gap of last five year?"

Rommond looked deeply into Brooklyn's eyes. "Don't waste the next five trying to bridge that gap."

Brooklyn bowed his head. "Thank you for this gift. You would make good Ootan."

"It was always yours," Rommond said. "I just had it for safekeeping."

"Then ... thank you for keeping it safe."

Rommond smiled. He hoped this small gesture would help Brooklyn reconnect with that lost part of himself, and show that the general really could trust him, that he had no reason to be afraid. Yet, for whatever peace that night gave, they knew that they would be setting out for the Wild North in the morning, a place where war was as common as sand, and where there were many things, and many people, to fear.

Chapter Five

THE WILD NORTH

The Wild North began eighteen miles north of Blackout. The land changed dramatically there, the flat sand plains exchanged for towering ridges and endless wastes. Some parts were so barren that even the sand did not stay there. All that was left was the dry, cracked earth. In other parts, the cacti reigned supreme, growing to immense sizes, standing like sentinels over the land. In others yet, the land was fertile, and many of the tribes fought for that sacred ground.

Between the Wild North and the Devil's March to the west of Blackout, they were the only things keeping the Regime from taking the Resistance strongholds in the west. The Iron Emperor had his Iron Wall, but the Resistance had a wall created by Nature—the only problem was that it stood against them as much as it stood against their enemies. Nature was neutral—she hated all of them equally.

The Silver Ghost rolled up slowly to the border. It was an unmanned border, with no one from either side of the war policing who came and who went. However, that did not mean it was unwatched. It was watched by the weather, and by other unseen eyes.

Few travelled there. There was barely any "there" to go to. Sometimes the lawless hid in that land, knowing the law would not follow, but the Wild North had its own kind of rules. The number one rule was: anything goes.

"This is it," Taberah said. "Beyond this point, you can forget our war."

"Easier said than done," Jacob responded.

"Oh, you'll forget it quick enough," Rommond said. "We could be fighting a different one here. Why did you think I wasn't keen to come here? I'd rather we focused on our own."

"Hell," Jacob said. "Next you'll be telling me ghost stories."

"Oh, we won't have to do much telling," Rommond replied. "The land here will show you. I used to be a doubter too. The land will make a believer out of you."

Jacob shuddered. "So, is this where people like me get out and walk back to Blackout?"

"This is where we say there's no going back."

The day waned, and the Silver Ghost roamed on, rocking and shaking as the land grew more rugged, like a mattress with many broken springs. Night drew its curtains, but the inhabitants of the warwagon had a difficult time falling asleep. They did not have to toss and turn; the vehicle did that for them. What dreams were had were disturbing ones, but those who could dream were fortunate, for many were forbidden slumber by the land.

Though Rommond was an adopted child of the land, thanks to his unintended marriage to Brooklyn, he did not sleep that night. It was neither the sand nor the soil that kept his eyes pinned open. He kept himself awake.

"Stop the wagon," Rommond called up to Taberah in the one-man cockpit. "There's someone out there."

The Silver Ghost ground to a halt, just metres before a figure. Though the night was dark, the silhouette of a man was clear. He stood still, very still, like another sentinel, blocking the path of the warwagon. All eyes were open now. Fear trumped fatigue.

"I'll go out," Taberah said, as she jumped down to the main deck.

"Are you crazy?" Jacob asked. "You don't know who that is? I thought you said this place is dangerous."

"I did," she said, "but I'm dangerous too."

"We're all going," Rommond said, jumping down from the last few rungs of the ladder. "Or I'm driving this thing over whoever's outside, and to hell with the consequences."

Taberah and Jacob left the vehicle, but Rommond stopped Brooklyn near the door. "You better stay here. We need someone to look after the wagon."

If it had been Whistler, he would have no doubt protested, but Brooklyn was not one to complain, and was not eager for adventure. Besides, Rommond was not one to listen to protests. He left quickly, and even more swiftly closed the door. There were two other doors on the other side, but before they entered the Wild North, the general made sure both were firmly locked.

The group walked slowly around the Silver

Ghost, pistols in hand, until they could see the silent, steady figure, staring blankly towards the warwagon. It stood in the middle of the dirt road, if those worn tracks could even be called a road.

"Who goes there?" Rommond shouted over.

The figure did not respond. Its clothes shuddered in the gentle breeze, but otherwise it stood perfectly still. The darkness disguised it. Whoever it was, it had the night as an ally.

"Sand got your tongue?" Jacob said.

They approached closer, treading carefully, with pistols cocked, watching the silhouette take form, until even the night could no longer hide it.

"That's no man," Taberah pointed out.

Rommond pulled the hat off the figure, revealing a straw head.

"A bit dry for crows," Jacob said.

Taberah and Rommond glanced about, turning their backs to one another, gazing off into the blackness all around. Jacob felt his own back was markedly exposed.

"The tribes don't put up things like this," Rommond said. He reached for the revolver on his belt, and pointed it and his pistol at opposing points in the shadow. If he had more hands, he might have pointed guns in all four directions—and yet still felt like maybe that was not enough.

"The bikers don't either," Taberah replied, moving her rifle back and forth across a steady arc.

"We're barely here five minutes and we've got creepy scarecrows," Jacob said, keeping his own gun close. "You weren't wrong about this place."

Taberah glanced back and forth. "I'm more concerned about what it's trying to scare away."

"Or *who's* doing the scaring," Rommond added. Jacob thought it must have been a very brave sort to try to scare the general.

Then, as if to answer Rommond's question, they turned and saw another figure to their left, seated in the shadows on a large slab of granite, which looked like a fallen remnant of an ancient monument. This reclining figure wore a long, deep blue coat, and a matching cowboy hat, similar to the scarecrow, but he carried a guitar, and his head was bowed, hiding his face.

"Howdy, soldiers," he said, tipping the brim of his hat. When he raised his head, Jacob could see that he wore what looked like a permanent gas mask over his mouth and nose, with pipes leading around on the right side to his back. Steam periodically puffed out of a vent on the left side of the mask. What part of his face was visible was cracked, more, it seemed, from the weather than from age, and his eyes were dark and grim, with a thin line of black around them, accentuating their grimness.

"Damn it, you startled me," Taberah said.

He strummed his guitar a single time. "It's what I do."

"Well, I'm glad it's just your voice startling me," she said. She turned to Rommond. "Give us a minute, would you?"

Rommond tipped his cap to the masked figure, before turning back to Taberah. "Take as long as you need." He hopped back into the warwagon, where it seemed like someone was peeping through a crack in one of the window shutters.

"I'm staying," Jacob said.

"You her bodyguard?" the man rasped.

"More like she's mine."

The mask did not show it, but Jacob was sure that the figure smiled. "Ain't that the truth."

Jacob could clearly see several pistols on show around the man's belt. It was what he could not see that worried him. He looked at Taberah. "So ... are you going to introduce us?"

"Now, where are my manners?" the masked man asked, taking the words slowly, letting his breath accentuate and deepen them, and the mask muffle them. He glanced about, as if he could find his manners in the barrels of his guns. "Some call me the Sandsweeper. Some call me the Coilhunter. Some call me the Masked Menace. But you, boy, you can call me *friend*." His eyes lit up with the word, and the grit in the man's throat made it sound anything but friendly.

All those titles were familiar to Jacob. He thought it was three different people. The Wanted posters made it seem like he was an army. He certainly had the munitions for one.

"Don't let him rattle you," Taberah said, slapping Jacob on the chest. "He's a big old softie, he is."

The man leant back, letting go of the guitar. "What can I say? Big Old Softie it is."

"What are you doing here, Nox?" she asked.

"What am *I* doing here?" Nox replied. He let his breath sound audibly at the end of every sentence, and it always seemed a little angry, enhanced by the vibration of the mask. "Some say this here land ain't got no sheriff ... but I'm the sheriff here. I've even got the badge." He flicked his finger against a buckled five-pointed star upon his breast, each prong a different colour.

"What's with the colours?" Jacob asked. Nox did not look like the kind of guy to wear a badge if it did not mean something. He also looked like the kind whose meaning would be grim.

"This used to be just four points, one for each type o' foe: the red for the tribesmen, when they ain't complyin'; blue for the bikers, when they ain't buyin'; green for the criminals, when they ain't tryin'; yellow for the Clockwork Commune, when they ain't dyin'; and black ... well, the black one's new, and it's for the demons ... pretty much all the time. I'd have painted it with blood, but everyone bleeds the same shade, and red ain't my favourite colour."

Given the many guns, Jacob was not so sure about that.

"Do you still have all your gadgets?" Taberah asked.

"Oh, I have 'em all right. Question is: is there a big enough prize for me to catch 'em with?"

"Ever heard of the Iron Emperor?" Jacob said.

It was muffled, but he heard the man humph. "I heard of 'im all right, but that's a war you're talkin' 'bout there, and I ain't no warrior."

"Neither am I," Jacob said, "and I'm still fighting in one. But if you're not a warrior, what are you then, if you don't mind me asking?"

"With this here pretty lady on your arm, I don't

mind at all. Some say I'm a bounty hunter—"

"And quite a good one at that," Taberah interjected.

He puffed out a cloud of smoke, and through the haze Jacob could see a ghost of a smile in his eyes, like the ghost of those he hunted.

"But some might take offence to that there remark," he said. "I hunt the wanted and the unwanted, whether that be criminals or bounty hunters. If I were just the latter, I'd be huntin' myself."

"Well, everyone needs a hobby," Jacob said.

"That's a quick tongue you got there, boy."

Jacob smirked. Nox might have had grizzled features, but Jacob suspected he was born that way. He did not so much as age as erode.

"Pity you ain't got the pistol draw to match."

"What makes you think I don't?" Jacob asked, and Taberah smiled. Beneath his hurt feelings, he was happy to see her smile, but he did not show it.

"Oh, I *know*," the hunter said. He suddenly drew his pistol and fired into the scrub. They heard the death cry of a rattlesnake. "Besides, you just told me you weren't no warrior, and if I were a bettin' man, I'd say you weren't no gunslinger either."

"I used to be a betting man," Jacob mused.

"Out here, boy, every night under the stars is a bet of life or death. If it isn't the tribes, it's the biker gangs. If it isn't the biker gangs, it's the Clockwork Commune. You got no metal to rob, they'll rob your bones instead. But if it isn't them that get ya, it'll be the sand or the sun or the scorpions." He looked at Taberah with that last comment. "Or it'll be the stars themselves."

"At least it won't be the rattlesnake," Jacob quipped.

"This one's a bit of a joker, eh?" Nox said coolly.

"Yes," Taberah said, "but *I* wasn't joking when I said you're the best I've seen. And I've seen a lot come and go." Jacob could see where she was going with this. He vaguely recalled her praising him before he was inadvertently recruited.

"Mostly go," the Coilhunter said. "But I ain't here to hunt praise."

"What are you doing this far south?" Taberah asked.

"What I'm always doin'," he said. "Puttin' the 'wild' back in the Wild North."

"Better than where we first met," Taberah said. She seemed suddenly unsettled.

"This is nature's graveyard, Taberah, and I'm the gravedigger."

Jacob humphed. "Seems like you're a lot of things."

"Careful, boy," Nox said, adjusting his badge. "Don't wanna have to make this up six."

"Pity black's taken," Jacob replied. "That's just my colour."

When Rommond returned to the Silver Ghost, he paused, as if something was amiss. He tapped his foot and looked at Brooklyn, who seemed a little nervous. Then he stared straight at one of the closed doors on the vehicle, and continued to rap the floor with his boot.

"Your mother will be very angry with you," he said.

There was no response.

"I will be too if you don't come out right now."

The door creaked open slowly, and Whistler stepped out, his shoulders hunched, his head bowed, his hands in his pockets, to disguise whatever mischief they were up to but moments before. He was not wearing his cap, so his reddish-brown curls covered his apologetic eyes.

Rommond folded his arms, careful not to crease his uniform. He shook his head, and sighed as he spoke. "What are we to do with you?"

Whistler bit his lip, and looked up while still keeping his head bowed, so that he stared through the prison bars of his hair. "Let me off with a warning?" he suggested.

The general guffawed in response. "You'd think we'd given enough of those." He paused as the laughter faded and the tension returned. "You'd think the Wild North was warning enough."

Whistler shrugged. For someone who wanted adventure, the Wild North was more of an invitation. The dangerous places, with the perilous names, always looked the most exciting on the maps.

"Tabs isn't going to like this one bit, you know."

Whistler grew defiant. "I don't care."

"You don't care how she feels?"

Whistler pursed his lips, refusing to answer.

"Brogan, it's not polite to ignore a question."

"I'm not ignoring it," he said. "Why should I care if *she* doesn't?"

49

"She cares, Brogan. You have to care to be angry."

Whistler shrugged again, feigning indifference, but his curls could not disguise the frustration in his face. He could not claim he did not care, because he was clearly angry himself.

"We're not far enough into the Wild North," the general said, "that we can't turn back and drop you off." He heard a disapproving *hmm* from Brooklyn. He was not the type to criticise openly, but Rommond knew his little signs and tells.

"I guess," Whistler pouted.

"We would lose time," Brooklyn said. "Time very valuable now."

Rommond screwed up his eyes. "Did *you* know about this?" he asked.

Brooklyn was never a very good liar. It was not a skill the spirits taught him. He needed some training with a certain smuggler.

"You lot have been around Jacob too long," the general said, shaking his head in disbelief. Had they been soldiers, he might have court-martialled them for insubordination. "We've got a bunch of smugglers and liars aboard now, a *lot* more than we need."

"We have ambassadors," Brooklyn corrected. "Ambassadors we need."

Rommond turned back to Whistler, wagging his index finger. "You better make a fine ambassador then, Brogan. I don't want you to make a fine corpse. Trust me, chap, Tabs doesn't either."

Nox barely budged from his stone seat, and Taberah and Jacob stood still as well. It was almost like a stand-off, except they were firing words instead of bullets. They might even have seemed like friendly words, but Jacob suspected that the Masked Menace was not in the business of making friends. It got in the way of his real line of work collecting bounties, for which he likely amassed a lot of enemies as well.

"There's a lot of *fine* bounties on Rommond's head," the Coilhunter said, nodding towards the warwagon, as if he was considering cashing in on one.

Taberah sighed. "Yes, he's lucky to be still alive."

"Oh, it ain't luck. I've combed this here waste from north to south, and east to west, and I ain't found no luck amongst the grains."

"Maybe you can help us," Taberah suggested.

There we go, Jacob thought. *So much for the foreplay.*

"You never really needed my help," the Coilhunter said. "And I ain't in the business of helpin' win a war. But maybe you can help me. Ya see, I'm here searchin' for someone else. Maybe you seen 'im. Maybe you saw 'im wormin' through the sands like a snake." He span his pistol, which still smoked from the previous shot.

"We haven't seen anyone out here," Taberah said. "We've just arrived."

"Keep your eyes peeled," Nox said, "or someone else'll peel 'em for ya."

"We better get back to the road," Taberah said.

Jacob was amused at how quickly she gave up. It did not seem like the Coilhunter was biting the bait. For her part, she was *all* about business, and it did not seem like there was a pay-off here.

"It's a long journey," Taberah added.

"Ain't that life." Nox paused, then patted what looked like several scrolls in his pocket. It did not take much to guess that they were Wanted posters. "Though I guess for some, it ain't that long."

"Before we go," Jacob said, as Taberah started to stroll back to the warwagon, "mind if I ask what happened?" He made a gesture like placing a gas mask on.

Nox let out a puff of smoke from the filter on his mask, which might have been the equivalent of a sigh. "No can do, boy," he rasped. "It'd give ya nightmares."

Part of Jacob shivered, but he tried to hide it. He had some doubts about Nox, but he did not doubt those words. "Fair enough. Well, see you around." He offered a mock salute.

"Consider this your sheriff's welcome," Nox replied. "People come here when they're tired of bein' hunted. Criminals. Murderers. Smugglers. People choose this place 'cause they think it ain't watched. But I've got two good eyes, see, and I'll be watchin'."

He pointed at Jacob, and gave a final strum of his guitar. A compartment opened up in it, and Jacob flinched, but instead of bullets it let out a thick smoke, which wafted up around the Coilhunter, until all that could be seen were his watchful eyes, and then nothing at all. When the fog faded, he was gone. Yet somehow it still felt like they were being watched.

Chapter Six

SILVER IN THE SAND

"You know a lot of strange folk," Jacob said to Taberah as they returned to the Silver Ghost.

"And you don't?" she asked, glancing back at him over her shoulder.

Jacob nodded. "I guess you're right." *Cala was enough strange for a lifetime.*

"Let's get this show on the road," Taberah called to Rommond.

"We're already up and running," Rommond called from the engine room, where they could hear him shovelling coal. "Just give it a minute to heat up."

As they waited, Brooklyn surveyed the interior. He held up a fallen red tapestry with finely woven threads. Many of them were on the ground or piled in a corner of the corridor. It did not seem like Taberah cared any more. It used to be a vessel fitting for a queen, but it seemed like she had abdicated the throne.

"This vehicle is very messy," Brooklyn said.

Taberah scoffed. "Don't tell me you've caught the same bug Rommond has."

"I heard that," Rommond called from the other room, and they heard him bang the shovel down in response, though he likely only placed it in its perfect place. "There's nothing wrong with a little order." They heard him sweeping up to prove the point. "This old boy could do with a right scrubbing. All these handles are so greasy I wish I was wearing gloves."

"This old *girl* is fine as she is," Taberah replied. "Sometimes you need a little dirt." She looked at Jacob, and he humphed in response.

Brooklyn ran his finger across one of the empty shelves running along the top of the corridor, which might have at one time housed books, were literature that did not praise the Iron Emperor not outlawed. The dust was thick there.

"Hard not to gather dust in a desert," Jacob said.

"I remember *you* were a little messy when I first met you," Taberah pointed out to Brooklyn. "Before Rommond programmed you."

Brooklyn looked to the ground, to where the dust had gathered. Then Jacob realised he was looking at his mechanical hand instead. *Maybe 'programmed' wasn't the right word*, he thought.

"I needed order in my life," Brooklyn said. "I needed meaning."

Jacob nodded. "I guess we all do."

"Okay," Rommond said with an exhausted sigh as he stepped out into the corridor. He brushed a dot of soot from his sleeve, and grumbled when it left a stain. "I've got this thing set up with enough fuel that we should be able to stay on auto-pilot for a while. Hopefully we'll get some sleep before we arrive in tribal territory, though I still think one of us should sleep in the cockpit just in case."

Rommond popped into the cockpit to push forward the gear-stick, then hopped back down as the warwagon chugged along slowly of its own accord. They retreated to the lounge area at the back of the warwagon, collapsing onto the cushioned benches that lined the walls. Even those were a little dusty, as if no one had relaxed on board the Silver Ghost for quite a while. Jacob did not mind the dust. He laid back, placing his hands behind his head, and yawned.

"Comfy," he said. "Maybe I'll sleep out here."

"What are these?" Brooklyn asked, holding up a pile of papers that were peeping out of a drawer beneath the bench. Jacob thought they made a familiar rustle.

Rommond glanced over. "Oh, they're nothing."

"Some of these are my designs," Brooklyn replied.

"I didn't mean *nothing* in that sense," the general said, twitching his moustache. "I meant they're not of much concern to us *right now*."

"They are for mechanical birds," the tribesman said.

"What, like that messenger one you sent out?" Jacob asked. "I wouldn't mind having one of those for a pet. At least you don't have to clean up after it."

"Only oil," Taberah said.

"No," Brooklyn replied. "Ones to sit in, ones to fly in."

"Remind me never to try that," Jacob commented, feeling nauseous from the thought of it alone. "The airship was bad enough. I'm not a religious man, by any stretch of the imagination, but I say if God wanted us to fly, he'd have given us wings."

"God may not have, but the spirits gave me these wings," Brooklyn said, holding up one of the diagrams displaying a wooden frame on wheels, something that looked like it would barely float, let alone fly.

"We never did get them to work," Rommond explained, taking out some shoe polish for his boots. "They could only stay in the air so long."

"I was not finished on them," Brooklyn said.

"Well, you'll have to leave that for another time. We've got problems on the ground to worry about. I think the war of the air is over. It's not the rustle of the wind that worries me. It's the rumble of the earthquake." He set one boot down with a thud, before moving on to the other.

Brooklyn was silent for a time, with the only the rumpling of pages to kill the quiet. "Why do these have Regime labels on them?"

The general sat up, and closed the little tin of shoe polish, before depositing it back in his coat pocket. "We found them in the Hope factory south of Blackout."

"You mean these are the papers I smuggled out?" Jacob asked. "I thought you said they were worthless."

"Worthless to our current efforts," Rommond said. "But it's better that they're in our hands instead of the Regime's. Though, to be honest, I think they probably have their hands full with us."

Rommond paused and stared at his boots, which sparkled in the low lamplight. He took off his cap, revealing his neatly trimmed chestnut hair, and ran the brim between his fingers; for a moment Jacob thought he was going to try polishing that as well.

Then the general let out a very audible sigh, and everyone perked up from their study or dozing. "Now," he said, with that same timbre he used to end a meeting, "before we continue any further, I think we need to sort out something. It's better we sort it here than when we visit the tribes."

Brooklyn stood up sharp, like one of Rommond's soldiers. "I think I will be in cockpit." The general nodded slightly to him, and Brooklyn quickly left the room.

Jacob wondered if maybe he should have used that excuse, but his curiosity would have kept him there. "What's wrong?" he asked.

"Nothing's wrong … per se."

"Just come out with it, Rommond," Taberah said.

"Tabs, I want you to be calm about this. We're a little too cramped for fire."

"It depends what *this* is."

Rommond sighed again. "Come out," he called. He placed his cap back on, as if readying himself for a battle.

It took a moment before there was any sign of stirring. Then the door of the nearby room on the left opened slightly.

"Fully out."

Whistler slunk into the room, looking as guilty as he did when he was almost caught stealing from Rommond's room aboard the Lifemaker. Jacob held back a chuckle. The others looked a little too sombre for his snickering.

"You idiot!" Taberah cried, jumping up from her seat.

"I'm not an idiot!" Whistler shouted back.

"Hell, Taberah," Jacob said, "lay off the kid."

"What do you know?" she barked, turning an accusatory finger upon him. "You think you're a father now? It takes more than giving in all the time to make a parent."

Jacob was about to give a smart-aleck response, but held his tongue. Riling her up was one thing. He could take it. But he knew who was getting the tongue-lashing tonight.

Taberah turned her fiery glare on Whistler. "You don't know how dangerous these lands are. You think it's bad under the Regime's rule, where the law comes heavy? You have no idea what it's like in this wasteland, where the law doesn't come at all."

"What about that coilhunter?" Jacob asked. "He said he was a kind of sheriff."

Her attention was stolen by Jacob once more, and with it went her rage. "Oh, he'll come looking for your killer all right, but only after he finds your corpse." She spat the words with all the venom in her, as if she was spitting on the killer, as if she could see the murder in her mind.

"Why do you even care what I do?" Whistler asked. The cage of his hair did little to hide the glisten in his eyes.

She turned back to the boy again, and her own eyes welled up. "Why do I care?" she asked, running her fingers through her hair. "Do you not think I've *always* cared? Do you not think that when I held you in the Order headquarters, that I didn't feel as though I too had been burned? I don't want to lose you, Brogan! I don't want to lose you like I lost … like I lost the others."

Whistler was shaking now, and very close to tears. It was only a quickly-fading sense of defiance that stopped the deluge now. "I'm sorry," he whimpered.

"Don't be sorry," Taberah said. She grabbed his shoulders suddenly and knelt down before him, pleading with him, and shaking him with every word that followed. "I want you to be safe."

They did not hug, as Jacob might have done. She held him, at a distance, like she held everyone, and he kept his arms pressed firmly to his torso, clenching his fists, even as she clutched his shoulders. She shook him, as if to wake him up, to make him see the dangers of the world, or make her own eyes see that he had not joined Elizah in eternal sleep. When she was not shaking him, he shook on his own. Though it was difficult to watch, and Rommond looked away awkwardly, Jacob could only imagine what it was like for either of them.

"I'll be safe," the boy said in time, as if those words were the only thing that could stop her shaking him. Maybe it was an empty promise, the kind of promise a boy could not keep, and one a mother could never fully believe. "I'll be safe."

But before he had fully finished the words, something struck the warwagon with a bang, dinting the metal just inches from Whistler's head. He jumped away, just as many more dints formed in the metal.

Rommond leapt up, pistol in hand, and Jacob glanced out the window on one side, then the other, but he could not see anything.

The general did not look outside. It seemed he knew what this phantom attacker was. "We need to get out of here," he said. "Help me ramp up the speed."

Jacob and Taberah joined him in the engine room, while Whistler loitered at the door, clearly eager to stay close, and just as eager to keep a distance from his mother. From the door he could keep one hand and foot on the ladder up to the cockpit, where he could hear Brooklyn pulling feverishly on the levers, and mumbling something to himself in his native tongue.

"I need off auto-pilot!" the tribesman shouted down.

"Brooklyn needs auto-pilot off!" Whistler repeated, glancing back and forward between the cockpit and the engine room.

Rommond span the wheels and dials with a frenzy, trying to set it back to manual, while Taberah and Jacob fed the furnace with a fury of their own. The warwagon picked up speed, but the metal continued to buckle under whatever assaulted them.

"Keep going!" Rommond cried, even to his own hands, which did not seem quick enough to crank the levers. Taberah joined him, readjusting controls he had just adjusted. Rommond might have helped make this vessel, but it was her baby, and Jacob hoped that meant she could operate it more effectively than him.

Jacob continued shovelling coal, until he thought he was burying the flame instead of feeding it. The last thing he wanted to do was bury anything.

There was a loud click, and then the warwagon

stuttered. "That's it," Taberah said. "We're back on manual."

"We might need some of your fancy driving," Rommond told Jacob.

Jacob raced outside, shuffling past Whistler, and launching himself up the ladder. He had squashed in there before with Soasa, and it was just as much a squeeze with Brooklyn. He seized the steering sticks and pushed them forward, only to feel the warwagon sputter and stop dead, as if the Silver Ghost had truly earned its name.

Jacob removed his hands from the sticks and looked at them as if they might be cursed. "What did I do?"

The furnace went dark in the engine room, and not a cog spun, nor a piston pumped. They heard Rommond and Taberah calling up to them, but in the cockpit everything was silent.

"The machine spirits are angry," Brooklyn whispered. "There is spirit-talker out there. He makes the spirits angry—angry at us."

Chapter Seven

WAGON WAR

Suddenly the machinery came to life, but it was not the life its maker ordained. It was a new life, instilled by another world. The dials went crazy, and the compass needle span, as if it had been sucked into the spirit plane, where there was no east or west, or north or south.

"We can't stay in here," Jacob declared, just as a level came down upon his head. He wrestled with it, but it became stiff and immovable, while others tried to reach out for him, like the material fingers of spectral forces.

Jacob reached for the door leading down to the rest of the warwagon, but it swiftly slammed shut. The wheel span into place, and no amount of force seemed to unlatch the lock. He banged on the hatch and yelled to Whistler. He heard the boy's faint responses, drowned out by what sounded like the engine room door also banging shut.

Jacob stood back up as the shutters on the windows below clapped like thunder. A single wheel of the vehicle span in place, alternating among them, rocking the warwagon like an earthquake. The lanterns dimmed and brightened, sending the shadows fleeing in all directions, as if they too were frightened of what assailed them.

Jacob turned to Brooklyn in frustration. "Well, you're the mystic of us lot. Can you not do something?"

Brooklyn could not hide the panic in his face. He held his hands before him, one human, one machine, both completely empty. "I … I do not know what to do."

"Talk to them!" Jacob urged. "I thought they listen to you."

Brooklyn shook his head. "They *do not* listen now."

"Well, we better do *something*," Jacob said, "or we'll be able to communicate with them a lot easier in the afterlife."

Whistler charged up the ladder as he saw it closing, but it was too late. He heard it bolt shut, and wondered for a moment if the others had sealed themselves inside. Maybe it was safer up there. That did not bode well for those left downstairs. Then he heard the engine room door squeaking, and he raced back down, just as Rommond and Taberah were running to the swinging door. It locked, and Whistler knew that they did not lock it. He heard Taberah roar in anger and thought maybe it was safer outside.

He listened to the muffled voices from both the engine room and the cockpit for a moment, but the distortion made them sound a little frightening, even a little bit demonic. He felt the sweat on his palms where he gripped the ladder tightly, and felt his heaving chest, and jumped at every bang, and yelped at every clatter. He might have been half-demon, but he felt the full fear that every human felt under such an overwhelming spirit assault.

Then he thought he saw a fleeting figure out of the corner of his eye. He turned sharply, but there was nothing there. Nothing there to see, at least—he could still feel something, could sense a presence. He gulped and looked up to the sealed hatch, and to the side to the sealed door, and wished he was not locked out alone.

He gulped again, trying to swallow the childish part of him, the part that made him want to run, to hide behind someone big and strong. He knew the others were counting on him, that he was the only person who could find some kind of override switch, if one even existed, or they might suffocate or starve in those locked cells, and it would be his fault. He knew he had to be a man and face whatever it was that was out there, even if he had to face it trembling.

Then he saw that fleeting figure again, and he shrieked. *It was nothing*, he told himself repeatedly in his head, but the more he said it, the more it seemed like the figure reappeared, and seemed a little more solid than it did before. It seemed small, like a young child, but he got the flash of a face in his mind, and it was his mother's. Her face, but not her frown or fiery eyes. He could have sworn he saw her in the engine room, but now he began to doubt himself, and he wondered if maybe she had gotten out in time.

"Mom," he said, immediately aware that he was saying it too softly, afraid that something else might answer, that something else might find him first. It was very dark, and though he knew the Silver Ghost well, it had always been well illuminated. With the lights out, it looked like an entirely different place, and he did not like that where he thought his mother was, it seemed the darkest place of all.

As he passed by one of the empty bedrooms, the door creaked open, and it did not seem so empty. The shadows congregated there, and he almost heard their whispers. He hurried past, glancing back over his shoulder, feeling his heart hurtling faster than his feet.

He halted suddenly when he thought he heard his name. *Brogan*, it said, and it might have been the voice of his mother, but he was not sure if he was just imagining it. He felt something touch his arm, and he cried out, shaking it from him as if it was a spider, but there was nothing there. His breathing was very heavy now, and he gasped for air. He rested his right hand on the cold silver of the hull as he tried to regain his breath, glancing about him at every shifting shadow, feeling like the familiar vessel had swiftly become an unfamiliar maze of haunted corridors, even though he knew there was just one long corridor, and three smaller ones leading off that to the doors.

Then he felt a sharp pain as the hull buckled inwards where his hand rested, and he shrieked and scampered back to the reassuring ladder, where he turned to see the door that faced it, and what looked like a painted face staring inside.

Then he felt a hand grab his shoulder.

* * *

Jacob tried every lever he could reach, but they actively resisted him. Even his strength combined with Brooklyn's could not make the door budge, and he thought even Soasa's effort might be fruitless. Indeed, it did not seem like Brooklyn was even trying. He paused between each struggle, closing his eyes and shaking his head. Jacob presumed it was a kind of meditation, but he did not think it was a very encouraging one.

"No luck?" Jacob asked.

"It does not feel like they can hear me."

"Let me give it a go," Jacob said, before addressing the four corners of the room, which were close enough that he could touch them, were Brooklyn not in the way. "Hey, spirits!" he called out, feeling like a fool, but thinking he would feel like a bigger one if he did not try something. "Can you hear us?"

The wheel that sealed the door shut span anti-clockwise, but by the time Jacob dived for it, it spun shut again and jammed. He slammed his fist on it.

"I'll take that as a *yes*," he said as he clambered back up. "And I'll take it you're toying with us too."

"You should not disrespect them," Brooklyn warned.

"Maybe they shouldn't disrespect us," Jacob suggested, before turning his attention to the spirits once more. "Can you let us free?"

There was silence. Even the wind outside seemed to hold its breath.

"I am getting something," Brooklyn said, closing his eyes. "I see us all chaining ourselves up."

Jacob scrunched his mouth. "I'm hoping that

vision is meant to be symbolic. I spent enough time in the Hold."

The shutters on the window clattered angrily.

"They do not like your words."

"Hey, you wanted me to play ambassador to the tribes," Jacob replied. "You didn't say anything about being a diplomat for ghosts."

The shutters went wild again.

Brooklyn opened his eyes. "They are ancient spirits," he said. "Not ghosts."

Jacob shrugged in frustration. "Hey, I don't know the lingo for this sort of thing. The closest I've gotten to the mystical and magical is selling those amulets full of … God knows what. I never asked. All of this stuff gives me the heebie-jeebies."

They heard a bang on the hatch, and they thought the spirits had begun another assault. The wheel span open, and Jacob charged to the door, only to find Taberah standing there, holding up a flickering lantern.

"So you found us," Jacob said, jamming himself between the door as it tried to close on them again. "We've just been here … meditating."

He clambered down, and Brooklyn followed swiftly, where they found Rommond and Whistler there, the former heaving with anger, the latter with fear.

"Every time I come here I end up in a broken vehicle," Rommond griped. "I hate these lands."

The lights flickered out, before slowly coming back on again.

"Probably best to keep that to yourself," Jacob said.

The hatch above opened suddenly, and a spanner fell down, smacking Jacob in the crown. "Hell!" he cried, rubbing his head. "*I* didn't say it!"

"We're not safe in here any more," Taberah said. "This place is a death trap if the enemy can control it. We need to get outside."

"If we can get the doors open," Jacob said, making sure to sidle away from the ladder. He knew there were plenty more tools in the cockpit. "Speaking of which, how did you get out of the engine room?" He pointed to the now resealed hatch. "We tried everything up there!"

Taberah glanced at him, but did not respond.

"If we go outside," Rommond said, "we'll face the tribesmen, and I have a feeling we'll be facing a lot of them."

"I'd rather face them," Taberah replied, holding up her rifle. "At least I can shoot *them*."

"What do these spirits even want with us?" Whistler asked.

"They're angry with me," Brooklyn lamented, raising his metal gauntlet as if it were a talisman of evil, summoning the wrath of the otherworld.

"How do you know that?" Rommond asked him.

"I can feel it … in my wires and bones."

Rommond shook his head, as if he could not accept that anyone or anything could be angry with Brooklyn. He turned to address the spirits. "Udanu! Who are you angry with?" he shouted, glancing about him.

The lights went out again, and then a few solitary flames lit up. In that weak light, it was clear to see that there was just a single figure illuminated: Taberah.

Chapter Eight

TOTEM

The light flooded Taberah's face, forcing the shadows to hide in the crevices of her eyes. Her features looked more distinct than ever, her cheekbones sharpened, her ruby lips defined. Her scarlet hair was tangled like writhing serpents. Though her eyes were not as fiery as they had once been, the flicker of the oil lamps reflected in them. She looked very grim, like someone telling ghost stories—or someone the ghost stories were about.

"I don't know why they're angry with *me*," she said.

Rommond seemed to be trying hard to hold his tongue.

"Oh, you think there's a reason?" she asked.

He still seemed reluctant to answer, like a spirit-board that would not spell out a name. "Well, you did dabble with all sorts in your younger days."

The light made it clear that Taberah was offended. "I didn't *dabble*," she said, "and if that's why they're angry, let's give them some real dabbling to worry about."

She turned and retreated into the shadows, but even as she did, the oil lanterns that had been previously doused ignited as she passed, illuminating her way. For a moment, Jacob was not sure if it was the spirits that did this or if it was her instead. Even as she reached the main door leading outside, and it swung open of its own accord, he still was not certain.

"Taberah!" Rommond growled after her.

"I don't fear these spirits," she replied as she stepped outside.

"It's not the spirits," the general said, "it's the tribes you should fear."

She did not listen, and they were left with little choice. They could not hole up in the warwagon, when every door and lock conspiring against them. They could face their fate outside, and they could fight, or they could surrender, or they could even become spirits of their own.

Rommond shook his head and grabbed his revolver. He flicked the barrel open and glanced at the bullets inside. It was fully loaded, six in number. He already knew this, but part of him suspected that the machine spirits might have stolen the ammunition. When the fight started, he wanted to be sure he got six kills.

"Come on," he said. "The spirit action is here, but the real action is outside."

They followed Taberah out into the desert, where the crescent of the moon acted as a lantern of its own. The Silver Ghost was visible in a thick ring of darkness, and out there in the shadow there might have been just empty sand, or there might have been a hundred spear-wielding tribesmen, or there might have been something else entirely, something they still would not have seen in the light.

Jacob felt something brush past him, and he tried to resist jumping. It might have been the wind, but the air was deathly still. Whistler stood close by, flinching every now and then. Rommond and Brooklyn stood to the side like sentinels, and though the spirits likely assailed them too, neither one of them moved an inch.

Rommond took his pistol from his belt and handed it to Brooklyn, who held it reluctantly in his metal gauntlet.

"You know I am not fighter," the tribesman said.

The general looked at him. "You better get in the spirit of fighting quick then."

Taberah's hair blew madly, and a vicious wind circled her, and only her, forcing the others to back away. It was as if a tornado had appeared around her, a dust devil without the dust. It was an angry wind, and the howl it made did not seem entirely the work of weather. Yet she stood there, in the eye of the storm, and she did not blink, and she did not baulk.

She reached inside her wine-coloured waistcoat and produced a little trinket, a crude wooden carving of a full-bodied woman with stunted arms and legs. It hung on a chain, and Taberah dangled it in front of her. Though the wind pulled at every part of her, tossing her hair and tugging her clothes, it did not touch the little wooden pendant, which hung deathly still in the tempest. Then the wind suddenly stopped, as if it had just seen what she held before her, and there was a different howl as something, or rather a host of somethings, an army of somethings, fled away in all directions, brushing past the others, setting all hair on end.

"Hell," Jacob said. "What was that?"

Whistler clung to his arm, not wanting to find out.

Taberah turned to them, still dangling the totem before her.

"Great Mother," Brooklyn said.

Whistler gave him a curious look.

"Where did you get that?" Brooklyn asked.

"Mudro thought it might be useful," she answered.

Rommond grumbled. "I wish that magician would let *me* in on his tricks."

"What is it?" Jacob asked, as Taberah handed the pendant to Brooklyn, who held it up for all of them to see. "Seems you make amulets to scare away all sorts of things."

"She did not make this," Brooklyn explained. "It is Muada-andulu, Mother-charm, which only Wachu Muada, Mother-clan, can make. It is forbidden to all others. It is totem of Great Mother, who birthed us all. We are all her children, even spirits. And naughty spirits flee at sight of Mother, or they will be scolded."

"Handy," Jacob said. "Though I guess it doesn't work for all naughty children." *I'm still here after all*, he thought. He winked at Whistler.

"You should not have this," Brooklyn told Taberah, his face graver than hers.

"It served its purpose," she said. "Mudro suspected we might face some resistance."

"Only Wachu Muada may use this," Brooklyn said. "It is forbidden."

"I follow my own laws," Taberah said. "Humans know it, and the demons know it too. The sooner the spirits learn that, the better off they'll be as well."

"This is not a world I wish to tamper in," Rommond said. He held up his gun. "I need a fight where *these* still work."

At that moment, a crowd of tribesman, armed with spears and bows, emerged from the shadows, the tips of their spears and arrows glinting in the moonlight.

"I guess you'll get one," Jacob said.

Chapter Nine

SURROUNDED

The leader of the attacking Udanudaga tribe stood forth, brandishing a ceremonial knife in one hand, and a string of small skulls in the other, with cogs for eyes. His long, dark hair was tied up, so that it almost looked like a tree was growing upon his head, the loose locks flowing down like leaves. His face was painted white, and his eyes were dark, as if it were just his own skull that sat there.

He shook the fetish of skulls menacingly at them. Brooklyn backed away, but the others stood strong. The leader chanted something, and the surrounding horde chanted the same verse in chorus. He chanted again, a different line this time, something in their native tongue, but the tribesmen were silent now. He chanted a third time, that first line again, and the crowd erupted once more. Drums sounded now, and it was clear that these were not the drums of dance, but war.

The tribesmen charged, yelling madly, waving their weapons in a frenzy. Rommond and Taberah fired off several shots, killing many of the attackers, but there were many more of them, and they were soon forced to turn to hand-to-hand combat. He always said that a soldier must still be a soldier in the battlefield of inches. And for that, Rommond did not just have a saying; he had a sword.

He slashed them with the edge of the blade and lashed them with the flat, wounding as many of them as possible in a single strike. Taberah bashed them with the butt of her rifle, striking them in the face, whacking them in the knees, and crushing them in places that hurt a lot more.

Brooklyn did not fight, and he never fired a shot, not because these were his people (his own had little love for the Udanudaga), but because his people fought not just *for* peace, but *with* peace. He could make weapons—he just could not fire them. The part that could, the machine part, the Regime part, he resisted, though it was difficult to resist. He kept close to the Silver Ghost, trying to commune with the spirits, but found them scattered, whispering among themselves about the wrath of the Great Mother.

Jacob tried to protect Whistler, ushering him behind him and pushing the boy back towards the warwagon, where no one could snatch him from behind. Two tribesmen approached carefully, raising their spears. Jacob was already out of bullets, and he did not think he could parry blows with his pistol. He had never considered himself much of a fighter, but he was quick on his feet. The problem was that he could not just dodge and duck—he had to be a shield as well.

The first spear flew forth, and Jacob edged out of the way, dragging Whistler along with him. The tip of the spear struck the warwagon, dinting the hull, for these were the diamond-tipped weapons of a tribe known for slaying metal. The second spear came in at the other side, and Jacob forced Whistler back the other way, where the first tribesman was still pulling out the tip of his spear.

Jacob saw his opportunity, and made himself into a weapon as well as a shield. He lunged at the first attacker, knocking him to the ground, and turning his spear on the second, where the diamond pierced flesh just as good as metal. As the second attacker fell, collapsing on Whistler, who cowered beneath the bloodied body, Jacob tried to wrestle the spear from the other tribesmen on the ground, failing to loosen the man's iron grip. So the smuggler kept one hand on the spear, to keep it in place, even as the tribesman tried to pull it from him, and used his other hand to fire punches, which were better than bullets, because they never ran out.

The horde hounded whoever the spirit-talker pointed at, and first he pointed at Taberah, but she beat them back, and she taunted them with her amulet, which beat back their will. Then the spirit-talker turned to Rommond, identifying him as the biggest physical threat, knowing that when a leader falls, the led fall with him.

While the tribesmen gathered around the general, and he swiped in a circle to keep them at bay, dripping sweat and blood, heaving and panting, one of the Udanudaga seized Brooklyn and threw him to the ground.

"Ootan!" the tribesman growled, before sitting

on top of him, holding the mechanic down. "You live with outsiders." He gripped Brooklyn's short hair tightly, almost ripping it from him. "You cut your hair." He then tore a piece from Brooklyn's blanket, holding it up. "Why wear this when you not honour your traditions?"

Brooklyn answered none of his attacker's questions. He did not fight or resist, though part of him wanted to. He kept that one tradition of peace, and knew that he might die for it.

"You are traitor!" the tribesman shouted, grabbing a rock and bashing Brooklyn in the face. "You conspire with walled-ones!" Another bash, another bruise. "You work with land-foulers!" Another ripple of pain, another cry. "With sky-darkeners!" It seemed then that the next strike might end the pain, and darken the sky for Brooklyn one last time. The rock struck once more, breaking through the skin, revealing the iron plating across part of Brooklyn's head, the part of him that was no longer human. The tribesman paused and backed away, before pointing a shaking finger at him and screaming, "The machine spirits have made you one of their own!"

Then something came over Brooklyn, and he felt suddenly very different. The memories of his people were replaced by different ones, and he felt like he was standing once again in the central plaza of Blackout, aiming the gatling gun strapped to his arm. He stood up and grabbed the Udanudaga by the throat with his metal hand, pushing him back against the warwagon. The tribesman struggled, but each kick just tightened the iron noose a little more, until he no longer had to worry about the fouling of the land or the darkening of the sky.

Brooklyn dropped the body, and he felt suddenly himself again, only a darker self, a self full of guilt and anguish. He had his old memories again, but now he had a new one: killing another person, killing them with his bear hands. But this metal gauntlet was not *his* hand. That metal plating in his head was not *his* skull. He was a mix of borrowed pieces, broken pieces. They fitted together, but they did not make him whole.

The tribesmen came from all directions, more than Rommond could fight in. While he blocked one attack, and broke another, two more came from behind. While he was parrying high, they beat him low. In time he was brought to his knees, and when he tried to get up, they knocked him down again. They threw themselves on top of him, bashing him with their hands. For a moment it seemed that he was overwhelmed, and his own cries were drowned out by theirs. Then they erupted off him, and he let out a roar like a volcano.

But they returned, tiring him, crowding in so that he did not have the space to use his sword. They piled on top of him again, crushing him beneath their weight, and though he struggled, he could not erupt again.

Yet through the gaps between the limbs, he saw the spirit-talker, with his eternal pointing. Rommond fumbled for his revolver, knowing he had just a single bullet left, the bullet he kept for their leader. He did not have a clear shot, but he did not need one. He fired towards the tip of a spear planted upside down in the sand. It bounced off, striking the warwagon, before bounding back towards the spirit-talker.

"No!" Brooklyn shouted, as he heard the familiar ricochet that Rommond was known for.

But it was too late. The bullet struck the spirit-talker, and he fell upon the ground. The fetish fell from his hand, and the skulls rolled across the sand, the cogs falling from their eyes.

Brooklyn shook his head. "The machine spirits are *very* angry."

The engine of the Silver Ghost ignited, and it almost sounded like an angered cry. It revved with rage, and the wheels span with hate. Rommond could hear it coming even underneath the soundproofing of the tribesmen's bodies, and he felt it too as one of the front wheels ran over them, crushing them. It was just metal. It did not have a heart. So, it did not care who it killed.

The tribesmen took the brunt of the impact. Several of them rolled off, clutching their arms, legs, or torsos, screaming out. And they screamed more as the Silver Ghost came by again. Others ran, abandoning their attack on Rommond, but the warwagon pinpointed the general with its lanterns, and it would not abandon the fight.

"Brooklyn, *do* something!" Rommond cried.

"I can't!" Brooklyn shouted back. "I call, but they do not listen. *You* do not listen. That link is gone, Rommond. It is gone!"

Rommond rolled out of the way of the next drive by, but he knew he could not do this for long. The Silver Ghost was built for speed. It had no guns, but now its wheels were its weapons, and its maker was about to be unmade.

Then Taberah stepped in front of Rommond, as the spinning wheels kicked up sand, and he was about to push her out of the way before that fateful hit, but the Silver Ghost halted mere inches from her, mere inches from the amulet she pressed towards it. The spirits fled again, and Taberah and Brooklyn helped the general to his feet.

"Brooklyn, you know I love you," Rommond said, "but you better get your act together with these spirits. You're our best ambassador there. We can't fight a war in two different worlds."

"Before this war is over," Taberah said, "we might have to."

Dawn broke, and the sun painted over the pigment of the night with its own dull shade of red. The sky looked as if blood had been spilt in the heavens as well as the earth, and while one eye of the gods closed, another brighter eye opened to watch the carnage.

The tribesmen were without a leader, but they were not without the will to fight. Though they were reduced in number, and many were tired and injured, they still outnumbered the others, and no sacred amulets would scare them away. They gathered around again, surrounding them, hounding them back towards the warwagon, as if they were offering them as sacrifice to it.

"Stay behind me, kid," Jacob said, ushering Whistler back once more.

The tribesmen closed in, and it did not seem like any amount of ammunition was enough for them. As it stood, the Resistance team had none.

"These are Udanudaga," Brooklyn said, as they drew closer, pointing a spear to his throat. "Slavers of *udanu*, of machine spirits. In league with Anganda."

"What does that mean?" Jacob asked, as another spear came dangerously close to his face.

"They do not take prisoners."

Taberah glared at her attackers. "Good."

Jacob gulped harshly. This was not how he expected to go out. He thought it was more likely that he would go down trying to breach the Iron Wall, the foundations of which he had helped to build as one of his many punishments for the crimes of his father. The image of the tracks flashed in his mind, where his childhood died. It was only fitting that his adult life die there too. But here? In the Wild North? *I'll soon be forgotten*, he thought. *Just another grain of sand.*

But the grains of sand that they all stood upon, that held them up, that cushioned their feet, were something more when they came together, when the wind took them in its invisible hands and tossed them to and fro, and turned them about, until they seemed alive, until it appeared as though there were other spirits working, speaking in the language of the weather.

As the Udanudaga closed in, pulling back their spears for the final strike, and as Jacob braced for that fateful moment, and still tried to block those blows

82

from hitting Whistler behind, dust devils seemed to spring up in the canyon to their right, and the whirling sands advanced towards them all—and mixed with the sound of the whirling, was the sound of stampeding hooves.

Chapter Ten

THE DUST RIDERS

The dust devils advanced at an incredible pace, taking all by surprise. Some of the Udanudaga fled at the sight of them, while others turned their spears in the direction of the charging pillars of dust, as if spear could hold back sand.

Jacob was about to seize the spear of one of the tribesmen, but Rommond held him back just in time as the whirling sand spirits sped by, crashing into the few Udanudaga who dared to face them. The wind was ferocious, even to those not directly in the dust devils' path, and the sand attacked all eyes, forcing Jacob to turn away and hold up his coat to shield his face, and his own body to shield Whistler.

Everything became suddenly very dim, as if dawn had been caught unaware, and was strangled by the persistence of the night. The sand kicked up so high that it partially blotted out the sun, at least to any who stood close enough to the spinning pillars. The haze was thick, making it hard to see much in front of their faces, and the stinging grit made any attempts to see even more difficult.

The sound was also ferocious, roaring in one ear and howling in the other. Jacob could hear people shouting, but the cries were muted. He only knew that they were shouts because he could hear them at all.

He stumbled with Whistler, pushing him back, trying to get closer to the Silver Ghost, to get some shelter, but neither of them could see where they were going, and the sand about their feet seemed to mount, as if the dust devils were feeding the dunes.

As they scrambled away, Jacob heard other noises like the neigh of horses, and he thought he was hearing things, until he saw what looked like the vague silhouette of horse-riders vanishing in and out of the sand twisters, and then he hoped he was seeing things.

At last they felt their way to the warwagon and hauled themselves inside, shaking the sand from them, rubbing their eyes and blinking furiously to dislodge the grit. They coughed up dust, until their lungs ached and their throats were raw.

"What was that?" Whistler asked mid-cough.

Jacob searched his coat for his canister. He gulped the whiskey down, and though it burned, it helped alleviate the drought. He almost felt like washing his eyes with it, but he knew that burn would not help at all.

"You're asking the wrong guy," Jacob said, handing Whistler the canister. "I'd offer you water, but this is all I've got."

Whistler reluctantly took the canister, just as Rommond, Brooklyn and Taberah stumbled inside.

"I was only minding it!" Whistler exclaimed.

Rommond and Taberah were wearing goggles,

but they still coughed up sand like all the rest of them. Brooklyn had his blanket over his head, and it was clear that Rommond led him to the warwagon or he would not have been able to see where he was going. The trio collapsed upon the floor, panting and wheezing.

"Phew!" Taberah said. "We got lucky there."

Rommond nodded, unearthing his canister of water and pouring some of it over his face before handing it to Brooklyn.

"You call that lucky?" Jacob asked, taking back his own canister from Whistler, who had been eagerly shoving it towards him since the others arrived. The smuggler swamped down another swig.

"We're still alive, aren't we?" Taberah replied.

"Until those dust devils come looking for more people to eat."

Rommond laughed. "You've never been up here before, have you, Jacob? Tabs is right. We got lucky here. Those are not just dust devils out there. Those are the Dust Riders."

"Losa Ariasa," Brooklyn said, sharing their tribal name.

"They're the most skilled of all the tribes' riders," Rommond explained, "so skilled that they can match the exact speed of one of those twisters, and they can hide in them, and they can even guide them, urging them along in any direction they will. Only the best of the best are out there. Those who aren't up to scratch … well, they don't survive the training."

Rommond seemed to admire this approach. Jacob was glad he did not quite apply the same strict rules for Resistance fighters.

Jacob tipped his canister to the general as a form of cheer. "Well, it's quite a cool idea."

"Where did you think we got the idea for Dustdelving from?" Rommond replied with a smile.

Chapter Eleven

THE LAST OF
THE GREEN GRASS

The Dust Riders never greeted them, and perhaps it was impossible to greet, what with the spinning sands about them, but Rommond gave a salute through one of the windows, before setting the warwagon back in motion, accompanied for a time by a galloping and a whirling, until the night crept in again, and those horsemen crept away.

Jacob watched as the thick sand gave way to a thin dust, which faded into a cracked earth, dotted here and there with patches of grass, until the warwagon rocked on healthy soil. The sight of the yellow and red turning to green was beautiful, and though Jacob was never much of a nature lover, nor much of an outdoorsman, he watched the shifting terrain and could not help but think back to what Altadas was like before the demons came.

"It's beautiful," Whistler said, peering out the window on the other side. There was no glass on those windows, but if there were, Jacob was certain that the boy's face would be pressed against it. Instead, he hung over the edge, dangling one arm, trying to feel the blades of grass as they whisked by. It took a moment for Jacob to realise that Whistler had probably never seen grass before. He was supposed to have been one of the Last, born just after the Harvest, but he was born even later than that, born to a human mother and a demon father, into a world of sand.

"Be careful," Jacob told him, as he glanced over to see the boy nearly completely out the window, his legs halfway in the air.

Whistler hauled himself back inside and perched himself on the edge of his seat, as if he was ready at any moment to dive back outside again.

"Why does it grow here?" the boy asked. "Does it rain here? Will we see rain?"

"I think Brooklyn would know more about that," Jacob said, "but as far as I'm aware, the tribes carry water from the wells for miles to manually water this land. It's why there's not much of it. It's the last of the green grass. They don't wait for the rain, because it doesn't fall often enough, or heavy enough. They tend to it every day."

Even as he spoke, Jacob could see figures in the distance, carrying long hollow wooden beams on their shoulders, with little holes every now and then in the frame, from which fell a trickle of water as they walked.

"Did your mother never bring you up here?" Jacob asked. It was a silly question. It might have looked pretty, even tranquil, but these lands were dangerous. Even he knew that. They were equally dangerous to humans and demons, which did not help Whistler's chances at all.

"No," Whistler said, pouting. "She came here a

few times, I think. I never really knew what she did. I asked once." He paused and looked outside again.

"And you didn't like the answer?"

"She told me not to ask again."

"So, who looked after you all these years?" Jacob questioned.

Whistler shrugged. "I spent a lot of time when I was younger with Uncle Alex, but he'd often go off on digs. He's an archaeologist. Well, was. Maybe he still is. I don't know if that's a real job any more."

"Yeah, I think the Regime outlawed it," Jacob mused. "Considered artefacts of anyone or anything but the Iron Emperor sacrilegious."

Whistler placed his chin on his hands, and furrowed his brow as he thought intently. "He was pretty cool. Alex, I mean."

Jacob smiled. "Yeah, didn't think you meant the Iron Emperor."

"He took me on some of his digs," the boy continued. "I really enjoyed it." He paused, and let out a tiny sigh. "I enjoyed the company." He took off his cap, letting the tangle of his auburn hair run rampant, and tapped the hat against the patches on his knees.

"Was there no one else?" Jacob asked him.

Whistler looked inside his empty hat. "Sometimes Rommond was there, but usually not. Brooklyn used to play with me when he could, when I was younger, but he was always getting called away to mend something, or the machine spirits would give him a new idea. I guess everyone was always busy."

"Well, you've got me now," Jacob said, grabbing the hat and placing it on his head. It was a tight fight, and probably made him look quite comical. He was counting on it.

Whistler giggled as he tried to take it back, which Jacob did not make easy. Though the boy was still very thin and slight of frame, there was a little bit more strength in him now, and Jacob was glad to see this.

When Whistler finally recovered the crumpled cap, half-panting and half-laughing, he looked at Jacob and said, "I just hope you don't get too busy too."

Rommond and Brooklyn sat in one of the cabins near the front, while Taberah retired to bed. The general stared outside, watching the sand turn to grass.

"Let's stop here a moment," Rommond ordered, though his tone was much softer than usual, so it sounded more like a plea.

He took the vehicle off auto-pilot, and knocked on Taberah's door.

"We're just popping out for a bit of air," he said.

There was no response, but he heard her turning in her sleep.

Jacob sauntered up. "What's up? Why are we stopping?"

"Just a personal matter," the general replied. "Do you mind giving us a moment and staying inside?"

"Sure," Jacob said. "Last time I went outside I almost got killed. You can consider me an agoraphobe now."

The general tipped his hat slightly, before leading Brooklyn outside, where the land seemed a lot more welcoming than it did before.

"Where are we going?" Brooklyn asked him.

"Just a little stroll."

It was a short walk, arm in arm, before they came across a wooden post in the ground, where the grass seemed to grow thicker than anywhere else, as if trying to hide that marker. Rommond crouched down and parted the blades of grass.

"This is where I thought I buried you," he said. "Well, part of you."

Brooklyn gathered his blanket around him tighter, yet it was not cold. "Why show me this?"

Rommond stood up and placed his hands on Brooklyn's shoulders. "Because I got you back, but I didn't get all of you. Somewhere deep inside you, you buried something else. You buried a part of yourself, and I can't dig that up."

Inside the Silver Ghost, as Taberah dozed, Jacob found one of the many munitions supplies, where he reloaded his two pistols, and took a few spare boxes of bullets just in case. Whistler stood nearby, just like he did when Jacob was rooting through his chest of coils, but now the currency was a lot more dangerous.

"What does it feel like?" the boy asked.

"What does what feel like? Holding a gun? Here, you try." Jacob held up one of the spare revolvers from the supply.

Whistler backed away, holding his hands up, palms out. "No, no. I don't want to try. I mean … what does it feel like … to … to kill someone?"

"Well, it doesn't feel good."

"For them or for you?"

"Both."

"So why do you do it?"

"Necessity."

Whistler frowned. "The world kind of sucks, doesn't it?"

"Yeah," Jacob replied. "But not all of it. That's why we fight. That's why we resist."

"I guess."

"Here. You may not like it, kid, but I think you should take one of these." He held up the revolver again, even as Whistler shook his head. "I hope you never need it, but if you do, I'd feel a lot better knowing you had something you could defend yourself with."

"But I don't want to fight."

"Neither do I, Whistler, but sometimes it isn't up to us."

Whistler looked at the gun with disapproval, his brow furrowed. Jacob shook it gently, trying to make him take it, and eventually the boy complied.

"It's heavy," he said.

"Did Rommond not let you hold a gun before?"

"He did, when I was younger," Whistler said, "but I kind of … dropped it."

"*Right*," Jacob said, regretting this a little already. "Well, just don't drop this one."

He showed Whistler how to use it, and use it safely, and store it even safer. It reminded him of his own father teaching him that same lesson when he was much younger than Whistler was, before he was hauled off to the workhouse. His father was a harsh teacher, and he could still feel the rapping of his knuckles when he missed a shot. Jacob knew there was no time for target practice with Whistler. Instead, he might have to practice on the real thing.

Chapter Twelve

THE COUNCIL OF THE LAND

The Silver Ghost arrived at its destination, deep in the heart of Ootana land, where a council had been called. The Ootana leader had received the message from the mechanical bird that Brooklyn sent, and all tribal leaders were summoned to the meeting, which was to take place in a large, dome-shaped, multicoloured tent that had long been used for the Councils of the Land.

The Resistance team departed the Silver Ghost and were led up to the pavilion, where several large tribesmen stood guard.

"Your weapons," the main guard said.

"What about them?" Rommond barked.

"Leave them outside."

"You've got plenty of your own," Jacob said, eyeing up the swords and spears. From what he could see of the congregations entering the tent through its three other entrances, they were well-armed too. It seemed that the Ootana were the only tribe that brought ambassadors instead of swords.

"Our land," the guard said, "our rules."

The general grumbled. "Whatever happened to *The Land is for all*?"

Jacob had never heard that phrase before. Any glance at the coloured territory claims on a map made it clear that neither the Regime nor the Resistance abided by it.

The guard peered inside the tent and shouted something in his native tongue. He did not sound pleased. Rommond kept his steely gaze until another guard, taller and broader, stepped out to greet him. Jacob found it amusing that they thought a bigger guard would make a difference.

"Rommond," the guard said. "So now we know why Council was called."

"Yes," the general replied. "Now, will you let us attend on time or make us late?"

"No weapons inside."

Taberah scoffed and shook her head.

The guard shoved his spear in Taberah's face. "You mock us?"

Rommond pushed the spear aside, and glared at the man. "Do *you* mock me?"

The guard thumped his chest, and the others followed suit. "We are Nusodee. Every Council called, we protect. That you attend, it shall not differ."

Rommond held up his revolver before the guards even had time to see. They readied their spears as he spoke. "This," he said, shaking the gun, "is like a hand to me. You're asking me to sever my own hand and leave it outside."

"You come with weapons, you come for war."

"Ah," the general said, "but I *did* come for war— but not with you."

The guards spoke to each other in their language,

to which the general rolled his eyes. Then they turned to Brooklyn.

"You," the larger guard said, before speaking something in the Ootana dialect.

Brooklyn whispered to Rommond. "This is custom. We *must* follow. We want them to give in to us, so we must give in to them. Diplomacy."

Rommond's moustache twitched, and he let out an audible, angry sigh. "Fair enough," he said, before taking several guns from their holsters and piling them up in a box beside the guards. He unstrapped his sword sheath from his thigh, making sure to wave the sword by the tribesmen's faces, before placing it gently in the growing pile of weapons. "As the saying goes," he told the guards as he passed inside, "you may disarm the man, but you still leave the greatest weapon behind—the man himself."

Brooklyn followed him in, and the guards did not even bother to search him. He was clearly an Ootan, and the Ootana never carried weapons. Jacob cast his two guns into the supply, but the guards stopped and searched him. He was not entirely surprised. *I would have searched me too.*

"Not sure what you're going to find down there," he said, as they patted his legs. They were rougher and more rigorous in response. "Didn't see you pat the general down like that. Afraid he might have taken a liking to you?"

The larger guard growled and pushed Jacob inside. It hurt, but not as much as those words clearly did. Jacob was just surprised that he was now not just taking damage for himself—he was taking it for the team.

Whistler came in behind Jacob, sulking.

"What's up?" Jacob asked. "Did they search you too?"

"No," the boy replied.

"Then what's the problem?"

"They didn't search me," Whistler said. "I could have had anything."

Jacob was no bouncer, but it was clear that Whistler was not hiding any weapons, unless he had bullets hiding in the tangle of his hair. But what nursed one person's pride wounded another's.

"You should be proud then," Jacob said.

"Why?" the boy asked.

"Because that makes you a *really* good smuggler. You can march right under their nose. I wish I could do that."

Whistler beamed.

Jacob could hear Taberah arguing with the guards outside. He knew for sure that she was hiding weapons. What he was not sure about was whether or not she would use them before she came inside.

They were led to a short, rotund woman, who sat cross-legged on a small round rug. Her hair was braided, and knotted into a variety of patterns, like a crown that Nature had ordained. She wore earthy brown clothes, with a blanket much like Brooklyn's over it, though it only had coloured buttons, not any of the cogs that covered his.

Brooklyn knelt before her and bowed his head. Rommond followed suit.

"I am Ala-usadi-ridalla," she said, crossing her arms before taking both of Rommond's hands in hers, and then uncrossing them, so that the general's were now crossed in turn.

"Maybe I'll just call you Ala," Jacob said.

She seemed offended. "Simple minds need simple names. You can call me Sitting Stone."

The Council was called quickly, partially due to Rommond urging Brooklyn to tell the tribes of their need of haste. Brooklyn seemed a little troubled, more than usual, and he did not seem at all confident talking to his people. Many of them looked disapprovingly on him, and some whispered about his short hair, while others whispered about the machine spirits.

In time, Rommond was invited to address the tribes.

"For many years, we have been at war," he told them. "This was not a war of our making. We were *forced* to fight. We were invaded by an enemy that sought to wipe us out. All of us. All tribes, whether of city or land."

"They leave us be," Aola, the leader of the Rasaoua tribe, said. Her people lived in the furthest north, under the shadow of the Gods' Teeth, a massive mountain range that at one time was covered in snow. They still wore their thick, woolly hides, but now it was merely ornamental, and a very uncomfortable tradition.

"For now," Rommond said.

"Your people brought them here," Aola said. "That is what Udanudaga say."

This annoyed many, especially among the Ootana.

"They once had seat at Land Council," Sitting Stone said. "Now they fight with Anganda at their side. We invited them to end old war and come here to talk. Then we could have heard what Udanudaga say. But they refused. So do not speak for them."

"I speak also for myself," Aola replied. "And I say, as we Rasaoua say, that the walled-ones brought the demons here, and that is why they fight them, and not us."

"Look," Jacob said. "I'm an outsider to all of this, but even I can see the damage the demons have done here. On the journey up, we saw the grass that you all keep alive. Where else can we see that grass? The Regime leaves you alone for now. They think you're beneath them, a lesser threat. If the Resistance is crushed, they won't ignore you any more."

Rommond nudged Brooklyn, as if he had prepared a speech, and thought now was the most opportune moment. Jacob was winging it, and it seemed to be working from the reactions on the tribespeople's faces, but the general was not leaving anything to chance. He came with the deck stacked in his favour.

Brooklyn stood up. "There are ten tribes."

"Eleven," Aola corrected.

Sitting Stone shook her head violently. "We do not count Anganda."

Aola smiled. "We do."

Rommond nudged Brooklyn again. If it had been him, he would have talked over the sparring tribal leaders. The message was not for them. It was for the people, because if they joined the cause, it was the people who would be laying down their lives.

"We speak many dialects," Brooklyn continued. "And we all have our own traditions, and our own sayings. But there is one saying we all know, one that comes from the Machu Muada: *it takes many blades of grass to make a field.*"

There was a flurry of nods to this.

Rommond rose quickly, adding, "And it takes more than one tree to make a forest. Do you even remember the forests we used to have here? Now we are lucky if we can even find a solitary tree. *We* did not do that. It was the Regime. They opened the gates to Hell, and let the fire through. We've been standing on that scorched earth ever since."

"We have to fight to reclaim our world," Taberah said, without standing up. "I've always fought, and I'll keep fighting. I'll fight *for* you, but will you fight *with* us?"

Rommond and Brooklyn sat back down as some of the tribespeople debated quietly among themselves. Some seemed steadfast in their disapproval, but others were not so sure. Rommond masked a tiny smile beneath his moustache. He could work with uncertainty. He could make them resolute.

He nudged Whistler now, who stood up self-consciously, holding a rolled-up map that the general had given him earlier, a little ace in the hole. There was a mixture of approval and dissent in the council at one so young being allowed to speak.

"Eh," the boy began, an unsteady start to mimic

the doubt among the audience. Whistler unfurled the map with a slight jitter in his hands, and held it up. "This is a map of the Iron Wall," he said. It showed the long stretch of track that ran from the port in the south right up to the mountainous ridges in the north. He pointed to the part at the top. "This part is where the grass is, where the land isn't covered in sand. I never saw the grass before I came up here. It's beautiful. And I'm sure it's beautiful there too, beneath the iron tracks. They dig there. They dig for riches. But they don't see the riches of the land."

The nods were more emphatic, and the sense of doubt was dissipating.

"Go on," Rommond urged. Their guard was dropping. They needed to go in for the kill.

"Eh, uh, I think … I think this land," Whistler said, pointing again to that strip of grassland close to the mountains, "I think this should be yours. I think you should be the caretakers, not them. I don't want to fight, but … but maybe we don't have a choice. Maybe we're not just fighting for us. Maybe we're fighting for the land."

The kill was in reach. Rommond shot up like a bullet.

"Though we will fight this war alone if we have to," he told the congregation, "we need every ally we can muster. To take down the Iron War, we need friends. We need you."

Sitting Stone shook her head. "No. You need ground. You need sky. You need water. You need fire. Us? No, you do not need us."

"To win this war, we need everyone to do their

part."

"Ootana do not win wars," she replied. "We win peace, or we lose peace. Everyone loses war."

"Then help us win peace," Jacob said.

The Mianachi tribe were more riled up than the others. They looked disapprovingly on the Ootana's gestures of peace, scoffing at their lack of strength. Their leader frequently interrupted the discussions to say, "We choose to live, so land dies. If land dies, we do not live." The more he said it, the more his people grew irate, raising their weapons for war.

"You know," Jacob said. "They're not going to stop until they conquer everything. That means you. That means the land. If you do nothing, you might as well rip that grass up with your own hands and smother the soil, because that's essentially what you'll be doing."

The Mianachi grimaced as he spoke, as if he was talking about disembowelling them. Some of them stood up, chanting in their tongue, and others from the opposing tribes joined them. In time there was enough amongst the congregation speaking a single word in a variety of dialects. *Toorasa. Trasat. Oosarta.* It all meant the same thing: War.

Chapter Thirteen

WAR DANCE

The chanting was so loud that it took some time before people realised that there were other voices, unfamiliar voices, shouting something else. The congregation fell silent, and all eyes turned to see members of the Anganda tribe entering the tent.

Their leader, whose skin was flayed, so that the red muscle was visible, marched up to Sitting Stone, who did not budge from her seat. He leant down to her, pressing his flayed face close to hers, until she looked away.

"I hear you call Land Council," he hissed. "It is no Council if you do not summon all tribes. Perching Tamba must have seat at table."

She turned back to him, and looked disapprovingly up and down at his mangled body. "You are no tribe, Perching Tamba. Anganda are disgraced Ootana, ashamed to even wear their skin."

"We were one," he replied. He had a way of talking that almost flayed the words, as if they could not leave his mouth without being despoiled.

"Ootana do not recognise Anganda," she said.

Perching Tamba smiled, revealing his razor-sharp teeth, whittled down into a point. For all their rhetoric against the so-called demons, the Anganda looked more like what they claimed to be fighting against.

Suddenly, the Anganda leader reached for the curved knife strapped to his belt, and swung it at Sitting Stone, who rolled back, dodging the blade. She ended on her feet, but she did not advance on her attacker. The other Anganda tribesmen unleashed a flurry of blades of all shapes and sizes, many of them more like scythes for tilling the land, now used to till the enemy instead. The Ootana evaded these attacks, never striking back, but the other more aggressive tribes dived at the Anganda, casting sword and spear, throwing knives and spitting darts. Amidst this chaos the Resistance members ducked and dodged, trying to scramble away.

Rommond was seized by one of the Anganda, who raised his blade as if to flay the general's skin, but he did not account for the Hawk's swift eyes and talon-like grip. Rommond stepped forward, blocking the attacking arm with a force that almost shattered the tribesman's wrist, but he continued on, striking the man across the neck, ducking from another blow, and knocking the Anganda to the ground with a ferocious uppercut to the chin. He shook the pain from his hand before seizing the tribesman's fallen blade.

He turned, just as another blade sliced by, chopping a button from his cuff. He glanced at the frayed thread with great displeasure, as if it were a wound of the flesh. Then he channelled his anger through his new-found sword, chopping off the arm of his attacker. "A stitch for a stitch," he said through gritted teeth.

Jacob and Whistler hid behind one of the large wooden beams supporting the tent, watching Rommond spinning and slicing, Taberah punching, and Brooklyn scurrying away.

"We have to do something," Whistler whispered.

"Yeah," Jacob said, dodging a dart. "I don't think a fist fight is going to work with this lot."

Whistler held up a pistol. "Maybe we can use this."

"Hell, where did you get that?"

"You gave it to me."

"How did you get it in here? You know what, never mind."

"I had it in my hat," the boy said.

"Sheesh, I'm glad I didn't pat you on the head." Jacob opened the barrel and sighed. "You know, kid, I'm not sure this'll be enough."

"What do you mean?"

"It's got two bullets. There's just too many of them. I mean, who would we even choose?"

At that moment, there was a flurry of noise in the tent, and they heard Rommond and Taberah struggling. Jacob thought that this was it, the "now or never" moment, before the Resistance and Order leaders were killed. He peeped out, readying the gun in his hand, but what he saw struck his resolve dead like a bullet of its own. There, at the entrance to the tent, stood Teller, the sun glinting off his bald head, the gaslight gleaming off his crooked smile.

Chapter Fourteen

ONE TOO MANY CHIEFTAINS

As Teller stood by the door, basking in his smugness, Jacob took aim. For all the trouble he had caused them, for everything he had done to him, to Whistler, to the entire Resistance, Jacob thought these two bullets were well-deserved. *Hell*, he thought, *he deserves a few more.*

Just as his finger clicked on the trigger, Perching Tamba dove at him, tackling him to the ground. The bullet fired, but missed its target, making Teller that little bit more smug. The gun slid away, and Jacob tried to shield himself from the Anganda leader's ferocious strikes.

"Walled-ones are weak!" the tribesman roared, digging his fists into Jacob's chest.

From the corner of his eye, Jacob could see Whistler picking up the gun. He held it up with both hands, aiming it at Perching Tamba. His hands shook, and both Whistler and Jacob closed their eyes. The bang seemed louder than most gunshots. It struck Perching Tamba in the shoulder, and the force of the recoil knocked Whistler to the ground.

The Anganda leader looked up at the boy and growled, before seizing Jacob by the ears and bashing his head upon the ground. Everything blackened for Jacob, but for Whistler, he could still see Perching Tamba's maddened eyes.

"I am going to enjoy flaying you," he said.

When Jacob came to, he found himself tied up, and so were the others, along with Sitting Stone and many of the other surviving tribespeople, though the latter were kept away from the Resistance hostages. It took a moment to realise that the bald betrayer really was standing there, that it was not just all a bad dream. On the other end of the large tent, Perching Tamba tormented some of the opposing tribes. For Rommond and his team, the torment was Teller.

"I thought you were dead," Rommond said.

"So did I, dear Edward," Teller replied, "what with all these *savages* about."

"You'll die soon enough," Taberah said, spitting the words at him.

Teller smiled. "It would want to be soon, for your sake, but Taberah, I am afraid I will disappoint you. You see, me … oh, I think I will live forever."

Taberah scoffed.

"Scoff all you will, but *marans* can change bodies."

Taberah eyed him up and down. "You should have changed yours a long time ago."

"How droll," Teller said, "but I am not actually *maran* yet."

"Yet?" Rommond asked.

"I am human, Edward, just like you. Well, maybe more than you."

"Not like me," the general replied. "You'll never

be like me. And do you hear that? That's the truth, something you appear to have great difficulty with, *demon*."

"I do not know why you resist, Edward. You could have this too. You could abandon your human frailties and let the Iron Alchemists do their work, transmuting one thing to another. And when you get old, you just do it all again. And when you run out of bodies here, you move to the next world, and the next, and you really can live forever."

"Then you'd have the sickness," Rommond said.

"He already does," Taberah added. "It's in his soul."

Teller chortled. "The Iron Plague is a small price to pay for eternal life, do you not think? Especially when iron is so abundant here. People partake of Hope even when they do not have to. A little boost now and then is a ... minor inconvenience."

"So you're not a demon in body," Rommond said, "just in your heart."

As Teller spoke, Jacob turned to Whistler, and it was clear from the boy's face that he had put it together: that it really was not his fault that he had not seen the demon in Teller—because he was actually human. He just desperately wanted to be something else. As Jacob looked at Teller now, he could not blame him.

Teller waxed poetic about his struggle to be accepted by the Anganda, how he had almost lost his life to the tribes, and how his exceptional speaking skills saved him. Perching Tamba was out of earshot, so Teller was very forthcoming about his position in the Regime, but he revealed that failure was not tolerated in the Iron Empire, "unlike the Resistance," a statement he made with much glee. Yet he was not so smug when he spoke of his salvation, of him redeeming himself in the eyes of the Iron Emperor by bringing him this prized catch, for which he would finally earn the great reward of being made like him. To the Anganda he promised a direct route to the man on the iron throne, so that they could finally kill the Devil, but once he got them there, he knew that they would all burn in Hell.

Teller rambled on, delighting in his ingenuity, revelling in the tale. He had spent months unable to breathe a word to anyone, plotting and planning, and finding his old enemies landing straight in his lap. That he wanted them to know how much trouble he had gone through was no surprise.

But the next part was.

There was an odd noise, like a quacking sound. Moments later the people inside the tent spotted a mechanical duck that had waddled in. It stopped and seemed to look at them with its little beady eyes, and everyone there looked at it in confusion.

Talk about a fish out of water, Jacob thought.

When Teller saw it, he said, "What in Heaven's name is—?"

It was not just an explosion. There was something in it that released a blinding flash, as if whoever had made it had discovered how to bottle lightning. Part of the tent ripped open from the blast, and there behind it stood the Coilhunter, his long coat billowing, his hat tipped down, his guitar strapped firmly to his back, his rifle held firmly in hand.

"Sorry to crash your party," he said, "but there's a guest here who isn't on the list." His voice grew suddenly darker. "He's on mine instead."

The Anganda leapt at him, but Nox threw a small orb at them, which burst, letting out three dozen tiny mechanical butterflies. They sensed movement, and flew towards the charging tribesmen, latching onto them, before releasing a noxious gas into their face. Some of the Anganda collapsed immediately, while others fought on towards the Coilhunter, trying to grab him with one hand, while swatting the wind-up insects with the other.

"Stay still!" Nox called over to Taberah, who was struggling with her bonds. She stopped, and the butterfly that was flapping its way over to her changed course.

Despite the fact that Nox marched on, the flying gas-canisters did not go for him. Jacob was no mechanic, but he knew it was not out of love for their master. As Nox walked, and the butterflies flapped, the tribesmen dropped like flies, until the Coilhunter was wading through a pile of bodies, kicking people out of his way.

One of the struggling tribesmen grabbed the tube leading from Nox's mask to his backpack, but he did not grab it for long. Nox had the man pinned to the ground quickly, pressing his boot into the Angand's neck.

"You gotta learn some manners, boy," Nox said. "Here, let me teach you." He struck him hard in the face with the butt of his rifle, knocking him out.

There was one person who did not attack: Teller. He was trying to flee until he heard Nox's warning to Taberah, and then he stopped mid-stride, keeping perfectly still, his back turned towards the Coilhunter.

"Reginald E. Teller," Nox said, drawing out the name, letting the words gather some of the grit in his throat, making the name sound like a death sentence. In many ways, it was.

The Coilhunter marched up to Teller. "Turn around," he said.

"I cannot do that," Teller said. "You made sure of that."

Nox tapped a button on a band strapped to his left wrist. The mechanical butterflies plummeted to the ground.

"There," Nox said. "I made sure you can turn now."

Teller turned very slowly. "Do not come near me. I have a bomb."

Nox must have smiled beneath that mask. "So do I."

Teller trembled. For all his brazen words to the Resistance fighters whose hands and legs were tied up tight, he no longer looked so confident. He wanted life eternal, but life did not want him.

"They will not pay you anything, Coilhunter. I am not r—"

"Oh, they'll pay," Nox interrupted. "I'll make sure of that."

The sweat poured from Teller's already well-oiled brow. "I can pay you more."

A puff of smoke came out of the filter in Nox's mask. "I've heard that line before. But, ya see, when I take up a contract—and every Wanted poster is a contract just waitin' for me to sign—I always follow through. This might seem like a lawless land, but I don't go around breakin' that unwritten law. So, yes, you'll pay more, but it won't be with coils."

"Please," Teller begged. "I … I have a family."

"No, he doesn't," Taberah yelled over.

"I have a future," Teller said. "I can … I can help you."

"He'll help tie you up."

Nox turned his head slightly and peered over the high collar of his coat. "Taberah, you got anything you wanna say to your captor here?"

"Only if I can say it with a knife."

"Sorry, love, it's nothin' personal, but I don't let anyone steal my kills."

At that moment, Teller darted away, but as quickly as he ran, Nox fired a small grappling hook, which embedded in the coward's skin. The Coilhunter reeled him in slowly like a fish.

"There's only one place you're going," he said. "To Hell."

He flicked his left arm, and a pistol popped out from his sleeve. He fired a single shot, right between the eyes. Teller did not have time to cry. He clattered off the ground.

Nox took out a Wanted poster from his pocket and cast it down beside Teller's body, where the blood crept towards it as if to claim the prize. On the paper was Teller's face, just like it had been on the poster he hung up inside the Silver Ghost, and there below it was the prize, a thousand coils, and below that the stamp of the Regime. It was a fake poster, just like Teller was a fake, but it might as well have been real, because it ended Teller's life.

Chapter Fifteen

PART OF THE TRIBE

The Coilhunter freed the captives quickly, and summoned his little pet butterflies back into their box. Something told Jacob that those were not the only pets he had.

"We could use a soldier like you," Rommond said.

"That's what every army keeps sayin'," Nox replied, "and I keep tellin' 'em I ain't one to be recruited. Some of us just weren't made for company. Some of us were always supposed to be lone wolves." He gestured to Jacob. "This one knows what I mean."

"Things have changed," Jacob replied, placing his hand on Whistler's shoulder. "You feel different when you're part of the pack."

"Sounds lovely, but I already had a family, and I'm still fightin' for 'em."

"Well, thank you for saving us," Taberah said, "and for killing Teller. He was supposed to be one of us, but he betrayed us."

"He was never one of us," Rommond stated.

Nox looked at the body. "Maybe you should have put up a Wanted poster then. I could've collected two bounties tonight."

"Well, we thought he was dead," Taberah replied.

"See, that's the difference between you and me. I don't think someone's dead till I've killed 'em myself. Well, though *I* won't fight your war," he added, pointing to Teller's body, "*he* won't fight it either."

The Coilhunter departed, dragging Teller's body with him. Jacob was not entirely sure what he was going to do with it, or if he would really get any money from the Regime. They might pay up just to know that he was dead, and not spilling secrets. Jacob just hoped there were no big secrets that the Resistance needed Teller to spill.

The attack by the Anganda rallied the Free Tribes together more than ever, and rallied them to the cause of the Resistance. Many saw the Anganda as a by-product of the Regime, granting that new tribe its *cause*, its reason for existence, but seeing them working with Teller made them wonder if the Anganda were secretly under the thumb of the Iron Emperor. Rommond knew that was not the case, that Teller had wormed his way among that tribe just as he had done with the Order, but he never revealed this. The lie sounded better. It helped blow the trumpets of war.

"I think we've delayed here long enough," the general said. "We need to head back to Blackout and make the final preparations for the attack on the Landquaker."

"Always in hurry," Sitting Stone said. "We must stay one more night. Many of us go not only to war, but to death. There is ritual that must be done. You must do it too."

* * *

The tribespeople made several giant bonfires, one for each of the tribes, and a larger central bonfire for the union of them, representing the Mother-clan, a few survivors of which were said to roam the lands. Some smaller fires were lit around these, some for the chieftains, some for the ancestors, and some for the spirits.

The drumming began almost immediately, and so did the dance. The dancers moved in a circle around the family of fires, keeping just one foot on the ground at any given time. They crouched in tight and low for some of the quick, low beats, then stretched their arms up high for the slower, louder ones, alternating their steps as they went. This mix of high and low was mirrored by their chants, and by the chorus of chants from the onlookers, all except the few Resistance members who did not know the words.

Sitting Stone walked around each of the fires in turn, casting feathers around them. Other chieftains followed, dropping a variety of objects, each of special importance to that particular tribe.

Then a few drops of rain fell from the sky. One of them caught Whistler on the forehead, and he was visibly surprised. Then many more drops came, until soon it was lashing down, the kind of rain that none of them, not even the tribespeople, had seen since before the Harvest.

"It's raining!" Whistler cried, turning around, his arms outstretched. His saturated hair stuck to his head and face, and the rain ran into his eyes. It soaked through his clothes, and yet he smiled as he was drenched. In an older time, people would have complained about this weather, but the people there were grateful for this experience, knowing well that it might be their last.

The rain doused the fires, one by one. It was strange to see them go out in order, not in unison. Sitting Stone told them that the spirits were accepting each tribes' sacrifice. Many of them would die in the coming battle. Their lives were exchanged for rain, so that the land could still be fed without their carers. One life for another.

Before the rain started, Brooklyn sat alone by one of the fires. Rommond would have sat with him, had he not been required at the chieftains' table. Brooklyn cast some little straw men into the fire, one for each of his people who had died in the recent attack. He dared not think of how many more little figures would be jumping into the flames when they launched their own attack against the railway gun.

He looked at his metal hand, and thought of straightening up the fingers. The hand complied, just like his human hand would. Likewise, he closed it into a fist. He tried all kinds of movements, and it seemed it answered to his mind. But something did not feel right. It almost felt like a ruse, like the hand was only complying so that he would let down his guard. He remembered the crushing of the Udanudag's neck, and knew that this was not a command he gave.

He made another straw man, spending more

time on it than the others, carefully crafting the arms and the legs, the head with its short hair, and the little hand with a tiny sliver of metal wrapped around it. He was crafting himself, a little miniature form. This was not how the tradition went. These straw men were for the dead. But for him, he felt it was already so.

What little wiring there was left in him did not matter. There were times when he felt like more of a machine. The spirits did not welcome him as one of their own. He was no longer a true Ootan. Even the Resistance no longer felt like a home to him. He had lost his connection. He was broken, and he felt like he could not be repaired. He felt like he had to be scrapped.

He cast the little figure into the fire, and the straw burned, and the metal burned, and whatever of the soul was captured in that form, was released to join the ancestors of the land, and finally found its home among the dead.

Chapter Sixteen

THE GATHERING

The journey back to Blackout was swift, helped by the wind created by the Dust Riders. They rode alongside the Silver Ghost, making it look more ghostly than ever in the shimmer of the sands. Some of the tribesmen boarded the warwagon, but others refused to be carried by machines, either distrusting the machine spirits which moved them or feeling it was disrespectful to them. They followed in wooden wagons, or on foot, and many of them struggled to keep up.

"Why are you called the Free Tribes?" Jacob asked Sitting Stone inside the Silver Ghost.

She smiled. "You are tribes that are not free. Imprisoned by walls of your buildings. Imprisoned by money. So many different captors."

"I suppose," Jacob said, "though sometimes thinking you're free is just another prison."

"You sound like Brooklyn," she said. "He philosopher."

Brooklyn blushed.

"Well, I don't think I am," Jacob replied.

"Ah, but still thinking. Philosophers always in their head."

* * *

They arrived at Blackout at midday, finding it bustling with activity. With Rommond gone, its citizens did not feel like they were under house arrest, and the Treasury made sure to avail of this opportunity, asserting its control. Ebronah made several speeches to the people from the balcony of her manor, urging them to pull together, and though they were different kinds of people, the kinds that "together" never seemed to apply to, they rallied to her words.

The Baroness was a master of ceremony, and she made sure to use Rommond's victorious return to the city to help fuel the atmosphere there, because she knew that they needed all these little successes when it seemed that failure loomed around every corner. The streets were lined with bunting of all colours, and the youth carried balloons, while overhead the Treasury's own hot air balloons floated. How things had changed—that was how the Treasury survived.

Communication was tightly monitored, so as to avoid any intelligence leaks to the Regime. Radios were, in most cases, prohibited, though a few were intentionally turned on at Mudro's camp to the south to further draw the enemy's attention to the seemingly massive army gathering there.

The Silver Ghost rolled into the city, with Rommond and company perched on the top, holding onto the shallow railing. The Dust Riders trotted through, and luckily for the city's people, they left the dust devils outside. A trail of tribesmen followed, like carriages of a train, until everyone gathered in the central plaza, where the field hospital had been replaced by a market faire.

There was music and celebration, and if the Regime had any spies there, they might have feared to report back the mood, for the mood in the east, in Ironhold and the other bastions of the Regime, was grim. At first the people of Blackout were suspicious, even frightened, of the tribespeople, but those suspicions and that fear was soon forgotten when they found that they all danced and drank the same.

"Enjoy today," Rommond told his people, as the Baroness invited him onto the stage, pinning another medal, the City Saviour, to his uniform. "Tomorrow will not be easy. Yet, for our enemy, it will not be easy either. We have fought them in the sands and the sea. We have fought them in the sky. We will continue to fight them, anywhere they assail us. In the bowels of the earth. In Heaven or Hell, there they will find us waiting, gun raised. When they march to us, they shall tremble in their stride. When they view us from afar, they shall want to stay there, out of reach. When they fire upon us, the shells shall be as rain."

The cheers were deafening, and perhaps even the Iron Emperor heard them in the east.

"Nice speech," Jacob whispered to the general as he stepped down.

"I wish I believed it," Rommond whispered back. "This rain will hurt. This rain will kill."

He did not stay for the celebrations, nor did any of his lieutenants. He holed himself up in the War Room, where they made last-minute preparations for the assault on the Iron Wall.

* * *

Later that day, Mudro joined them, and he seemed the least celebratory of them all.

"She's gone," the doctor said, limping up to them.

"What do you mean?" Rommond asked. "Who's gone?"

"Alakovi," Mudro said. "She left, not long after you did. She didn't help with the decoys. Many of the Vixens went with her."

"Damn it!" Rommond shouted. "We gain new allies, but we lose old ones."

"Speaking of allies," Taberah said, bringing someone into the room.

Rommond stood up sharply. "You," he growled.

Jacob was not sure who he was, until Whistler reached up and whispered into his ear. "That's the Crocodile. That's General Leadman."

Chapter Seventeen

THE CROCODILE

General Leadman was an older man than Rommond, with thick grey hair, but not a whisker on his mouth, and none upon his massive square jaw, which was unquestionably his most prominent feature, and what gave him his much-detested nickname. He was the kind of man who would not just berate you; he would grind you between his teeth. He was taller than Rommond, and quite a bit more plump, but he still dressed as finely, brandishing just as many medals—though Rommond would say that he earned his in half the time.

"Clear the room," Rommond told the others when Leadman was brought in. They left without protest, but some of them pressed their ears against the door.

"Fancy seeing you here," Rommond said. "I thought you were on vacation."

"You know there's no vacation from the war, Rommond."

"*I* know that," Rommond said, pointing to himself. "But who's been kicking back in Copperfort all these years? What made you come here? What made you pop your head out of the sand?"

"The rumours."

"The rumours of what?"

"That the tide is turning."

"Well, the tide has turned because some of us have been busy at sea, while you've been basking on the beach. That's why facts for us are only rumours to you."

Leadman had a granite face, but the anger could be seen through the cracks. "You should have a little bit more respect, Rommond. Let me remind you that I outrank you."

"Only in years."

"Let's get down to brass tax," Leadman said. "We don't like each other. That's been the case since the trenches. But we don't have to like each other. All we have to do is recognise the benefits of a mutual relationship."

"Go on."

"I haven't been idle while you were busy fighting your war, Rommond. Copperfort is a bastion now, more than it ever was, more than Goldwall was."

Rommond eyed him coldly. "Goldwall fell."

"But Copperfort is still standing."

"For how long?"

"I haven't ignored the threats we face."

"No, you sided with the enemy."

"While it was convenient to do so, yes."

"Ever the politician," Rommond said.

He had another name, which was not so pretty. The troops in the trenches came up with it, calling him the Crocodile. His large jaw always seemed ready to snap shut, so they never called him it to his face.

"We both plot and plan, Rommond," Leadman said. "Don't pretend you aren't just as much a schemer as I am. I'm just a little bit more honest about it."

"Go on then. Tell me your latest *scheme*."

"When I signed my agreement with the Iron Empire, the Resistance was *losing* this war. Now I see that the tide is turning, and I want to ensure that when the sand settles, I still retain a *prominent* place."

"If you built a sandcastle, the shifting winds can be very dangerous."

"Indeed," Leadman said. "But my castle isn't made of sand, nor is my army. While your landships were depleted, mine have only grown. Sure, we used Brooklyn's designs, which my agents secured, but it's not just the quality that matters; it's the quantity. And I have both."

"Then why don't you join the fight?"

"I intend to," Leadman said. "The question is: which side do I fight on? If I fight for you, with you, then I want you to guarantee me a place at the head of the table when we're enjoying the, as it were, post-war feast."

"You mean, you want be the new Iron Emperor."

"A Lead Emperor, if you will, but really the metal does not matter."

"I can't guarantee that," Rommond said, "and I think the days of empires are over."

"You're the face of the Resistance, Rommond. You have sway. If you tell people to follow me, they will follow. Call it an empire, a kingdom, or anything you will, so long as the people call me *leader*."

Rommond sighed. "That's asking a lot."

"You're asking for more," Leadman replied, prodding the table with his index finger. "You're asking me to risk everything to join the fight."

"I'm asking you to risk a little to help win the war."

"It's all about perspective, isn't it, Rommond?" Leadman asked. "And perspective's pretty much all about politics. What will you do when the war is over? You're a war-time leader, Rommond. I'm a leader for all seasons."

"Well, we've only got war and summer now, so it seems you'll have to wait."

"I can wait, Rommond. The question is, can you deliver when the waiting is over?"

"I don't know," Rommond said. "What if I can't?"

"Then I might have to consider *other* options. At present, I rule Copperfort, but if I pitched in with the Iron Empire to help quell this … rebellion, I could rule a lot more. It's no good just getting power. You have to keep it too."

"But what legacy would you leave? Humanity will eventually die out. There will be no one to sing your praises."

"If I am not here to hear them, what does it matter?"

"That is very short-sighted," Rommond said.

"Perhaps, but I bet that, of the two of us, I'll live the longer life."

"So you would sell your soul to the Devil, that you might be crowned a king of Hell."

"Or you could crown me a king of whatever new Heaven you intend to create. The option is yours. Be an angel, Rommond."

Rommond rubbed his fingers across his moustache. There were more bristles there than there were soldiers left in his army. The siege of the Iron Wall was about to get under way, and though Leadman was an opportunist, Rommond could not help but feel that he needed to be one as well.

"I'll think about it," he reluctantly said.

"Don't think too long," Leadman replied. "The tides are *always* turning."

When Leadman left, as smugly as he could, Rommond called for Taberah, and her alone.

"You know Leadman," Rommond said.

"I sure do."

"He wants me to promise to crown him king when we topple the Iron Emperor."

"So, promise it to him."

"The problem is," Rommond said, "I'm not sure I can keep that promise. I'm not sure I even want to. I think the people deserve a real leader, not an opportunistic coward like him."

"Then lie to him," she said. "Pledge whatever you need to get him to pledge his troops. Dangle the crown for him. He'll never wear it."

Chapter Eighteen

THE IRON MEDICINE

While the general and other plotters and planners got to work, Jacob relaxed a moment before the next big job, knowing well that it might be his last. He managed to get back into his old room at The Olive Inn, and found the book *The Essential Guide to Minerals* there, where he hid his smuggled amulets. He brought it down to the bar. With Blackout in Resistance control, it did not need hiding any more. He opened the book at the bar, and was surprised to find it contained something extra: a small red pouch containing five coils.

The money I gave Soasa, he thought. *God, I wish she'd gotten her patch of land.* In a way, she did. She was buried there now.

"Didn't take you for the readin' type," the landlord said.

"Everyone needs a hobby," Jacob replied, closing the book and patting the cover. "I guess 'minerals' is mine."

"You sure it isn't alcohol?" Gus asked, topping up the whiskey glass.

"A guy can have two hobbies."

"So he can."

"What about a girl?" Lorelai asked, stepping up to the bar.

Jacob smiled. "A girl can have anything she wants."

"I wonder if that smooth-talking is you or the drink," she said. "Maybe you can be a little smoother and get me one."

Jacob humphed. "You heard the lady," he said to Gus.

"A gin and tonic, please."

Gus nodded. "You got it, doll." He poured her the drink.

Jacob took out the bag of coils and slid one across the counter.

"Back to the riches now, are we?" Gus asked.

"Not quite," he said. "More like a parting gift. Might be the last one I get." He slid another coil over. "That should cover the whiskey too."

"It should," Gus said, "and you'd get a few for that, but you still owe me for the room."

"I'll add you to my will. You might get to cash in on it quick enough."

"Used to think of retiring," the landlord said, "but pouring drinks isn't so bad compared to what some people are doing."

"Drinking them isn't so bad either," Jacob said, taking another swig.

Gus chuckled as he walked away, throwing his towel over his shoulder. They heard him moving kegs in the back room. Jacob was not exactly sure why. There was no one else in there, and the cobwebs suggested there had not been for days.

"So, what brings you to this fine establishment?" Jacob asked Lorelai. "The free gin?"

Lorelai smiled. "No, I just think I need a drink after patching up Brooklyn. He had a nasty head wound. Pity the general won't let me stitch him up. I could tell he had some injuries too."

Jacob showed his bruised knuckles. "Don't we all."

"So, why are you here?" she asked. "Drowning your sorrows?"

"Boredom."

"That's what all the drunks say."

"No," Jacob said, faking a wobble in his seat. "We slur it."

"Surely you can't be that bored with that kid chasing you around. Is he your son?"

"What, Whistler? No." He took a bigger swig this time. "I don't have any kids. Well, there was Elizah, but … she's … she's not here any more."

"I can relate," she said, downing half her drink in one long gulp. "He was around Whistler's age when he died. He's why I became a nurse."

"Sorry to hear that. I mean, about your kid, not the nurse part. You make a great nurse."

She sighed. "No matter how many I save, I keep wishing I could have saved him. I guess I keep thinking that if maybe I save a thousand lives, it will somehow make up for it. I know it won't, but I keep trying all the same."

"Well, don't stop trying. We could do with more people sealing wounds instead of making them."

She nodded, before reaching into her inside coat

pocket. "You don't mind if I … ?"

"Go ahead," Jacob said. "Mudro's already stunk up the place."

She took out a little pouch and dipped her finger into the white powder inside, before licking it up.

"What are you doing?" Jacob asked. "I thought you meant a pipe or something. You can't take that stuff here."

She looked up at him. "Where else will I take it? I'm not exactly going to retreat to a Hope-house."

Jacob tutted. "Why is it that most of the women I meet are taking Hope?"

"Maybe you meet a lot of demons."

Jacob raised an eyebrow. "One or two."

She ingested more of the powder, which even now looked a little tempting to Jacob. To many, Hope was the real demon. Once it bit you, it never let go.

"Well, I'd rather you didn't take it around me," Jacob said, looking away, looking out the window to the sky, where even the clouds reminded him of the drug.

"Don't tell me it offends you."

"It doesn't."

"You're not an addict, are you?"

"Not an addict, no," he said. "Are you?"

"My body needs it, Jacob Black. But it's different for me, for us 'demons'."

"How? I never really *got* your … food."

Lorelai laughed. "Food. Yeah. It's not as simple as that. It's more like medicine."

"Medicine for what?"

"We've got a sickness, Jacob," she said, sighing as

she spoke, and there were years of labour, of toil and struggle, of searching for a cure, in that sigh. "The Iron Plague. It struck our people over five hundred years ago. We hoped to find a cure, but every time it seemed to go away, it would just come back again— and it would come back stronger. We lost so many to it. You don't want to see what happens when we don't take our medicine. Our skin blackens and hardens. It almost turns into iron. And it flakes off, and people just … people just fall apart. Right in front of you. Bits just …" She sighed again. "It's no wonder we got the name 'demon'. Some of our people, some of the most desperate, came through the Portal, and they looked so monstrous, how could anyone think they were anything else?"

"Hell," Jacob said. He could not really think of anything else to say. *Sorry* just did not cut it.

"Hell," Lorelai mused. "You say that's where we came from, but it isn't true. Our original world was called Mes Marana. You call us demons, but we have our own name for our people. You are humans, and we are *marans*. No matter how many lands and realms we've been through in our endless search, we still know in our hearts who we are, and where we hail from."

"So why impersonate humans?"

"To fit in, I guess."

Jacob scoffed. "Hell, you haven't done a very good job of that. Look at this world now. If you had been here before the Harvest, you wouldn't recognise the place."

"I *was* here before the Harvest," she replied. "I

was a Pilgrim, a scout sent to survey this world, to decide if it was a good place to come."

"You better not let Rommond or Taberah hear you say that, because it kind of sounds like you helped spell our doom."

"I helped my people slow down our own."

"But you still haven't got a cure," he said. "And, you know what, there are people like Rommond who might say that your people are our disease. You're wiping us out, faster than that Iron Plague is doing to you."

"We all do what we have to for survival."

"So then maybe the general's right not to let you sew him up. I mean, what's to stop you trying to kill him?

She scowled. "I'm trying to *save* people. This whole thing has just … gotten completely out of hand. I'm not the only one who thinks. Many *marans* now question the Iron Emperor. They just don't do it openly, because that's when you get the kind of knock on your door that you don't want to get."

"Damn," Jacob said. "Well, I think *I* need another drink." He paused. "Here, before I make Gus any richer," he added, flicking a coil into the air before passing it over to her. "Tell me something. What does this inscription mean?"

"I don't think you want to know."

"Try me."

She held the coil up to the light, and read the words. "*Alantra, dorsk ianalan calol. Dorsktra ianalan, dorsk ru calol.* It's *maran* for: To heal, we must conquer illness. To conquer illness, we must conquer all."

"Doesn't that say a lot?" Jacob asked.

"I don't know. What does it say?"

"I think it says it all. Your Iron Emperor ... well, he's a warlord."

Lorelai sighed. "We've been fighting a very long time. All this war. All these people dead and dying. I've been trying to do my bit to help alleviate the pain. But it just keeps coming."

"Then this war has to end, and I don't think it'll end with the Iron Emperor still sitting on his throne. So long as he's leading, he'll lead your people into war. I get that you're looking for a cure, but five hundred years of war hasn't unearthed one."

"Maybe he's just not looking hard enough," she said.

"Maybe he isn't looking at all."

Lorelai placed the coil back down on the counter, the back side up, so that the Iron Emperor's eternal gaze could not be seen. Maybe he really was not looking for a cure, but to many who saw his visage on that currency, it definitely felt like he was always looking.

The door creaked open, and in stepped a man who looked more than a little familiar. Jacob looked at him from over his shoulder. He was a little surprised to see anyone frequenting this place at all, but he was more surprised by the man's attire. He looked awfully like a sky pirate.

"Jacob Black," the man said.

Jacob turned around fully. He glanced at the gun

strapped to his thigh. He did not feel up for a fight. He did not think the whiskey would help.

"Who's asking?"

"My name doesn't matter," the pirate said. "I'm here for El Abra."

"He's dead."

"That's why I'm here."

Jacob knew it. Revenge did not have a time of day or a place of residence. It could come anywhere at any time.

The pirate reached inside his pocket, and Jacob reached for his gun.

"You can put that away," the pirate said. "I didn't come here for a fight."

"What's that you've got?" Jacob asked.

The pirate pulled a little wooden toy horse from his pocket, and held it up. "This is something the Snake wanted you to have." He placed it on the counter next to Jacob.

"Seems you got a birthday you're not telling us about," Lorelai said. "First the coils, now this. Maybe I should have baked a cake."

Those were the kind of lines Jacob might have said, and might have laughed at, were his focus not stolen by that little mahogany horse on the counter. He picked it up. His eyes welled immediately. Who knew that the dam could be broken so easily, with such a little thing? He was only a little thing himself when he last saw it.

"He kept it," Jacob said. "He kept it all these years. We could not play with the toys we were forced to make. So one day he stole one from the conveyor belt.

He got in *so* much trouble. Olbaron beat us anyway, but he got ten times the beating then. They searched high and low, but they couldn't find it. I thought he'd gotten rid of it."

"Well," the pirate said. "Now it's yours. It took me quite a while to find you. I came here a few days back, but they said you left. I figured you'd be back at some point. When you're in El Abra's crew, you quickly learn about honour. He made me promise to get this to you, and I had to honour my word."

"Thank you," Jacob said. "It means a lot."

"I only wish he was still around. The seas and the skies are a lot quieter now."

"Why did he do it?" Jacob asked. "I mean, why did he join the battle against the Black Barge?"

"I guess he felt he had to honour his friendship with you. He took a nasty wound from that landship, but he doesn't hold grudges, not like the Masked Menace up north. He knew he was going to die. I guess he felt he should do something good before he went out. He knew it was his swansong. It's why he gave me this task before he set sail that final time."

Jacob stared at the little wooden horse. He did not know what to say. He was struggling to stop himself from crying. For so many years, he was a slave. Now he was free, but he still felt like the chains wrapped around his heart.

"Anyway, good luck, Mr. Black," the pirate said. "There's rumours going 'round that you's are taking on the Iron Wall. El Abra never was one for the land. He used to say it was cursed, and I suppose after the Harvest it kind of was. Hopefully you have better luck than he did, and hopefully that little trinket is worth something to you."

In a shop, it was not worth even an eight of a coil, but it meant so much more to Jacob. He stared at it as the pirate patted him once on the back and left the inn. He turned it around, remembering how he had to turn thousands of them around each day. Then his eye caught the dull shine of the coil on the counter. He pulled it over, and heard the sound of it in his mind.

"You know, I guess there's a reason I like the chink so much," he said. "It buries the memory of another metal sound, the chink of an iron key in an iron lock, trapping me inside the tiny room I slept in when I was in the workhouse. *The* room, not *my* room. There was nothing there that was mine, not even the hours of the day, when I slaved away, and not even the hours of the night, when I dreamt I was still a slave of the system. This is why I don't like to stay in small rooms now, because for all my efforts to make my fortune, to pay and buy my way out of the system, I sometimes feel like the chains have never severed. They might have been broken from my feet, but not from my heart.

"But then I met these people—Whistler, Taberah, Rommond—and they showed me that maybe I'm bringing those chains around with me. Maybe there's something comforting in the feel of the manacle, because it keeps you tethered, tells you where you are, limits where you can go, so you don't wander, and you can't get lost. That shackle is called fear. Fear of the unknown. Fear of love. I lost my family once, but

I found a new one in the Resistance."

He had not quite realised that the tears were streaming down his face. When he noticed them, he blushed and looked away. He was glad the inn was empty. People went there to drown their own sorrows, not to drown in his.

Lorelai placed her hand on his and forced a smile.

"And you," Jacob said, wiping the final tears away. "I guess you're part of the family now too."

She reached in and tried to kiss him, but he backed away. "Woah," he said, holding out his hands.

She bit her lip. "Well, this is awkward. I thought … never mind."

"Sorry, I didn't mean to give you the wrong impression. I'm a one-woman man."

"The red-head. Is that your woman?" she asked.

"Yeah. Well … kind of."

"You go for the crazy ones then."

Jacob smirked. "You should see the other one."

Chapter Nineteen

PROJECT TRIDENT

By the time Mudro made it back to the decoy deployment, he knew they were already late to roll out. He gave them a final once-over as two of Rommond's lieutenants stared through spyglasses into the distance. They were new lieutenants, only recently promoted, and the extra pips on their uniforms did little to hide their fear.

The decoys were arrayed upon a giant wooden platform, one hundred metres square. It was propped up on many tracks salvaged from old landships, and the platform itself was covered with sand, making it virtually imperceptible from a distance.

Mudro gave the order and watched as the platform rolled forward. It went at a snail's pace, but that did not matter. In fact, that was a good thing. The enemy only had to see an advance. Mudro did not want them seeing the decoys up close. Without the Copper Vixens, he was really short on his promised manpower, forcing him and his team to slap together the fake landships as quick as possible. Some of the paint was still wet, though the sun would make short work of that.

The platform rumbled forward, and because it was

on real tracks, it made an audible rumble, just like real landships would, and because it was also powered by steam, fed by two crewmen who shovelled coal inside a furnace disguised as yet another landship, smoke billowed into the air, and it came up through fake flutes and chimney stacks, enhancing the deception.

Mudro sat perched in the back of a truck that trailed behind the false platoons. The lieutenants were there to join him, as were the handful of soldiers left with them. A few men propped themselves inside the decoy landships, popping their heads out of the hatches and making overly dramatic signalling gestures to add a little authenticity to the trick. It was all a marvellous ploy, but Mudro was not keen to judge it just yet—the real judge was the audience, and he did not yet hear the applause.

Mudro knew that at this pace it would take an hour before they were visible enough to the enemy, and by that stage they risked the iron ire of the Landquaker. If the Regime had moved the railway gun down to the south to shore up those defences, defences it did not really need, then a single shell could obliterate Mudro's phantom host. On the stage, under a single spotlight, sleight of hand was usually quick. Distraction with one hand, the real action with the other. But on the battlefield, where the sun was the spotlight, illuminating all, the sleight of hand was painfully slow. Worse yet was *being* the distraction. If the hand was caught, the audience booed, and Mudro knew that the Regime's heckles would be the sound of launching shells.

* * *

In Blackout, Rommond drew large red arrows on the battle map, all pointing to the east, where a stamp read: Project Trident. It was a new map, with revised markings, for a new army and a revised plan.

"This will be a three-pronged attack," he said. "Mudro's decoys should have already begun rolling out. They need the extra time. Taberah's team will set out next, with the help of the Dust Riders, following the northern trails, where hopefully we can secure a carriage train."

"Then we will take north," Sitting Stone said. "Their reserves will crumble."

"Good," Leadman remarked. "We'll have enough to face with the Landquaker. We don't need them shoring up the Gate."

"The rest of us," Rommond continued, "which is now a decent number with Leadman's support, will lead the central prong. We're throwing most of our forces there, because it needs to look like that's our main objective, to outgun the greatest gun this world has ever seen. All three prongs are sharpened, and now we just need to thrust the trident into place. In the south, we will distract them. In the centre, we will deceive them. In the north, we will destroy them."

"What if Taberah's team fail?" Leadman asked. "I never did have much faith in her."

"Well, I do," Rommond said, "and she has the best of the best as a boarding party."

"The best of the best?" Leadman wondered. "How come *you* don't have them?"

"I'm the one holding the trident."

"Well," Leadman said. "I'll pick it up if you let it

fall."

The grand planning ended, and each tactician turned to the little details with their crew. The secret mission in the north was the most valuable of them all, so that is where Rommond spent much of his attention.

Jacob was back in uniform—a Regime uniform. The general made him try it on, and shook his head in disapproval.

"Notice anything?" Rommond asked.

"What? How dashing I look?"

"Give me a salute."

Jacob complied.

"No. A Regime salute."

Jacob followed suit, placing his hand on his left shoulder. "Ah," he said, when he did not feel the patch with the Regime emblem there. He reached to his other shoulder, feeling the patch there instead.

"Dear Lord, I thought we had these made up to exact specifications," Rommond griped. "Get me a sewing needle."

"I'll do it," Lorelai said. "I'm good at sewing things up."

"Make sure it's done right then," the general said. "And while you're at it, check for any other oversights."

"Yes," Taberah added. "You should be good at that. You've seen a lot of Regime uniforms in your time."

Lorelai bit her lip as Rommond and Taberah left. She got working straight away on the patch.

"Quite the volunteer," Jacob teased. "Or were you just looking for an opportunity to rub my shoulder?"

She prodded him with the tip of the needle, and Jacob cried out.

"That's one hell of a bedside manner you got there," he said. He smirked to himself. "Or one pretty tiny pitchfork."

"Ha ha," Lorelai replied, drawing out the words. "It's all devils and demons with you, isn't it?"

"Hey, I'm not the one shovelling Hope down my gob."

Rommond met with each of the people on Taberah's team, walking them through the plan. He met them as a group, and then one by one, going over everything in meticulous detail. There was no opportunity for a screw-up, and he made sure they were aware of that. He also made sure that they knew that they might have to carry out the plan alone.

When Rommond visited Taberah, she was not happy with the choice of who was on her team.

"I don't trust her," she said, "and I'm surprised you do."

"Well, I'm surprised you don't see this for what it is—a tactical decision."

"What do you mean?"

"I've heard rumours that the Regime have ways of telling who's human or demon," the general explained. "It seems they couldn't tell in Blackout, but that was mostly under Treasury rule, and I'm not taking any chances with the Iron Wall. So we need a few more demons on the team. Lorelai is, as you might put it, *useful*."

"So, is that why you want Brogan to come too?"

she asked. "You know I don't approve."

"I hate to say it, Tabs, but that demon blood in him could save our lives. But it's not just about that. The Regime implemented new rules a few years back that require Field Commanders to take cadets. If we don't have someone young enough to be a cadet on the team, it will look suspicious."

"Given who we've got," she replied, "I think we're already going to look suspicious."

"Everything's a risk in this world, Tabs," Rommond said. "Even just being born. But I want to mitigate as many of the risks as possible. That's why for you, Tabs, I have an extra task."

He peeped his head outside, then closed the door slowly, making sure that no one could hear what it was.

The general's next stop was Brooklyn, and he had an extra task for him too.

"Brooklyn, before you go," Rommond said, "can you do me a favour?"

"Anything."

"How many trucks do we have left?"

"Two, not counting the one Mudro has. We salvaged all we could from Regime supply here."

Rommond turned his attention to the Long Spyglass, perched on the walls of the city. "It's not going to do much good up there, now, is it?"

"You mean—"

"Will two trucks be enough?"

"I had not thought of it."

"Well, think about it now," Rommond said. "Will

two trucks be enough?"

"It's heavy," Brooklyn said, "so I'm concerned about the sand. I could maybe put some tracks on the back truck, where it will take the most weight. But we're out of tracks. I'd have to take them from one of the landships."

"Take them then," Rommond said. "The talons of the Hawk are nothing without his eyes."

Chapter Twenty

THE CENTRAL PRONG

The gates of Blackout opened, and out of the city issued several dozen landships of all shapes and sizes, from some of Brooklyn's first designs to his latest. Leadman even had one that looked a little like the Hopebreaker, but it was not as fast, and Rommond was certain that it did not pack the same firepower.

"Whatever happened to yours?" Leadman asked him just before the signal was given.

Rommond responded with a cool glare. "The real Hopebreaker isn't made of metal. It's made of flesh," he added, gesturing to himself.

The platoons formed into a convoy, rolling out in single file to help disguise their profile from enemy eyes. Rommond's platoon was noticeably tiny: just five landships, two of which were not in great shape. He heard them creaking along beside him, and it was not a reassuring sound.

The general sat in the back of one of the trucks, where the Long Spyglass was fitted. Brooklyn worked overtime to get it ready, and faced some frustration as the lens needed readjusting.

"Lutgard," Rommond said.

"Yes, General?"

"Keep an eye on the formation, will you?"

"Of course, General. Is anything the matter?"

Rommond grumbled. "I don't trust Leadman."

"None of the boys do either."

"I can't help but wonder if this is all a ruse, if he's working with the Regime. At any moment the central prong of the trident could turn back upon us."

"Not to give you more to worry about, General, but if he's working with the Regime, then they likely know our entire plan. It could reverse all three prongs."

"Not our *entire* plan," Rommond said.

Lutgard nodded, but eyed him curiously. Rommond thought it better if he kept his best cards close to his chest.

As they headed further into the desert, Rommond looked into the Long Spyglass, scouring the railway in the east. He could not see any sign of the Landquaker, which meant it was either far south or far north, further than the magnification reached. He turned the scope with a creak to either side. He saw Mudro's moving charade in the south, and it looked convincing. In the north, he just saw a haze of sand, and that was reassuring. He turned the spyglass back to the railway, and still could not see anything. He was growing nervous now. If it was in the south, that was great news, but if it was in the north, where Taberah's team was hastening, it was the worst news of all.

He stared into the spyglass for an hour, until sleep began to stare back at him. He had not slept well the night before. No one did on the eve of battle. Then, just as slumber almost had him, he saw something travelling swiftly from the corner of his right eye. He turned the spyglass to see it, and there it was: the Landquaker in all its might and majesty, thundering along those rails, its gun pointing forward, away from the landships. It would not point that way for long.

Rommond watched it grow in size, looking at all the little details, the little swirls and motifs that he and Brooklyn had painted on together, that were Brooklyn's tribal stamp, and his artistic affront to the Regime's minimalistic style. He also saw that the vessel was now overlayed with the emblem of the Regime, that black square upon a red cross, all angular, without a curve in sight. Its red frame was enhanced by rust. Rommond was certain that the rust would not impede its dreadful firepower, or its tremendous speed along those well-maintained tracks. There were regular inspections by smaller trains and carriages, one of which Rommond was counting on Jacob and company to commandeer.

Then the moment came when he no longer needed the spyglass to see the railway gun. There it was on the horizon, a minuscule figure with a monstrous payload. As soon as that moment came, he knew the battle was on. The platoons split apart, changing formation, abandoning the winding serpent for a wall of their own. They kept a reasonable distance from one another, but Rommond knew it would not be enough.

The first shell came down with an ear-rending whistle, and an eye-roasting burst of light. By the time

Rommond's eyes adjusted, he saw smoke billowing to his left, where the wrecks of two landships smouldered. He was just glad it was not from his platoon. He could not afford to lose a single one. Not yet.

The second shell hurtled down at the head of Leadman's forces, casting one of the landships into the air. The others swerved to avoid it, and they were glad they were in Brooklyn's newer models then, which did not take so long to turn.

A third and fourth shell landed in quick succession, showing that the Landquaker's barrel had rotated fully into place, allowing full use of the loading mechanism, with all the enhancements that Brooklyn had once made. The shells exploded at the front of the formation, missing the landships, but scouring the land and casting up thick clouds of smoke.

Another shell struck the landship just in front of the trucks bearing the Long Spyglass and Rommond, casting the landship up and spinning it back towards them. Rommond ducked, but the spyglass was struck, sending the barrel spinning off on its own. The back truck toppled over, and the general tumbled into the sand. The front truck stopped, and the driver turned to beckon to him.

"Drive!" Rommond shouted, gesturing forward. "Drive!"

But another shell came down upon the motionless truck, making sure that everyone inside was motionless too. The general sighed and shook his head. Some troops let their compassion overcome their training. They forgot his oft-used words: *Forward is the only direction. For your feet. For your eyes. For your gun.*

He kept close to the toppled truck at the back, where that driver was still alive. "I never thought I'd have to walk to the Iron Wall," Rommond said.

"Maybe we should wait here," the driver replied, reluctant to move from his seat. "Maybe help will come."

Rommond rummaged through the back of the truck, pulling out a rifle. "You can stay here if you want, Ollie," he said. "I'm still pushing forward."

Chapter Twenty-one

THE MASQUERADE MARCH

The Silver Ghost had spent much of the day taking the Covered Trails to the north, a series of shallow canyons which might have at one time housed a river. These were old smuggling routes which Jacob knew well. Yet the team did not rely solely on the sandy walls to hide them, but used the cover of the Dust Riders too. The shutters of the windows were firmly sealed, but even then the sand crept in, and some of the crew kept their goggles on, and others wore their gas masks too.

In time, the warwagon halted on an outcropping overlooking Fort Landlock, the northernmost end of the Iron Wall, where the rails ended inside a colossal docking bay carved into the side of the mountain. It was digging that cavern which first led the Resistance to the discovery of Glass, and then the Glassfinder Project that resulted in the contraceptive amulets. Now the Glass mines were turned into iron ones, feeding the Regime's industry of war as much as it fed its people.

Taberah and Jacob poked spyglasses out of one of the windows. Though their shield of sand still somewhat obscured their view, they could see several small supply trains entering and leaving the docking bay, switching tracks and switching crews. Under the Regime's control, the Landquaker was in operation twenty-four hours of the day, never making use of the docking bay that the Resistance had made for it, and it needed constant resupplying, both of crew, food, and ammunition. There were different storage trains for each of these duties, colour-coded in blue, yellow and red respectively. Rommond's plan was to hijack one of the yellow ones, on the assumption that the food train would offer the least resistance, but Taberah thought that the red train was a better choice—even if it was a challenge to secure, it would give them extra ammunition to take over the railway gun.

"It doesn't look like we'll have to worry much about waiting," Jacob said. He could see the constant rotation of colours, and several supply trains were lined up, some rearing to go, and others opening up for new supplies. A steady stream of soldiers marched to and fro, and even from this vantage point, Jacob could hear their methodical beat, almost as mechanical as the Iron Guard.

"I still think red is a better choice," Taberah said.

"It suits you," Jacob replied, nodding to her fiery hair, "but I'd rather fight some loaves of bread and leave the real battle till the Landquaker. Besides, I don't think we should be changing Rommond's plans now."

"Funny that," she said, "how you've become suddenly so good at taking orders."

Jacob gave a mock salute. "Guess I'm a good

soldier now."

"Well, I hope you've kept some of those smuggling skills," she replied. "Getting us on board is *your* job. Once we're in, you can leave the soldiering to me."

The Silver Ghost withdrew from its vantage point and parked at a safe distance, away from prying eyes. Being that close to the enemy made everyone on edge, and made them think that there were many more eyes out there just waiting to pry.

Brooklyn drove a rickety Mark I landship behind, the kind the Regime adopted at the attack on the Hope factory, but he parked it even further back than the Silver Ghost, to avoid any potential mishaps of the two vehicles being seen together. It was also a noisy machine, and everything about this hijacking, this daylight robbery, needed to go quietly.

Inside the Silver Ghost, Jacob changed into his Regime uniform. He had received a promotion, with another pip upon the shoulder, and another medal, and after the success in Blackout, he felt he deserved it. He was also well aware that the Regime might be on to them by now, that the disguise might not be as convincing as he thought. Yet, as he stared in the mirror, adjusting his belt, he felt a shiver down his spine at the thought of how easy it might have been to switch sides. In the early days of the war there were a lot of mutineers, a lot of turncoats, switching allegiance as easily as the Treasury or Leadman did. It was an unsettling thought, but it also brought another: that there might be some among the enemy that did, or wanted to do, the same.

"What do you think?" Whistler asked, stepping into the room. His uniform was a much better fit this time. Lorelai spent some of the drive putting her sewing skills to use, taking up the trouser legs and arms. She did not see it as a chore. It beat sewing on severed limbs.

"Looking snazzy," Jacob said.

Whistler smiled, but he buried it just as quickly. "Only, I wish it was a Resistance one."

"Trust me," Lorelai said as she entered the room, "you don't want to march in there in one of those."

"Besides," Jacob added, "I haven't got a Resistance uniform either. Maybe no uniforms can do us guys justice. If you're smuggling something into a city, you wear their style of garb, not your own."

"You look good," Lorelai said.

"Thanks. Can't say I'm not partial to the nurse's uniform either."

She smiled, and self-consciously adjusted her long white skirt. "If we had more time, I could have made you one."

Jacob smirked. "Maybe later."

"Okay, I'll see you guys in a minute. I just want to check Brooklyn's wounds. I think he'll need a little bit more make-up to hide the scars."

She left the room, and Whistler looked out the door, watching her leave. He dangled his foot for a moment, and opened his mouth several times to say something, before exhaling noisily when he could not find the words.

Jacob raised an eyebrow. "What is it, kid?"

"Do you like her?" Whistler asked.

"What, Lorelai? Yeah, she's okay."

"More than … more than my mom?"

"Taberah's never just okay. She's hot or cold, fire or ice."

"Yeah."

"Well, kid, don't worry. I think I like extremes."

They met with Brooklyn outside his landship, where he was dressed in another Regime uniform, labelled as a mechanic. He wore gloves to disguise his mechanical hand.

"We must move quickly," Brooklyn said, looking to his chronometer. "We are already late."

They parted with the Dust Riders, who waited in the canyon for the rest of the tribal troops. Their slow march helped give the Resistance team a chance to infiltrate the base, right before the tribespeople would assault it. Jacob did not want to get caught up in that battle, because then they would be forced to attack the tribes or blow their cover. Either way, they would lose.

The team squashed aboard the Mark I landship, which chugged along, spitting soot and spewing steam. Brooklyn had an odd way of driving, which seemed a lot more intuitive than most. He never looked through the viewports. He seemed to be able to feel the ground beneath, feel it through the metal, through the tracks, as if the vehicle were an extension of him. In some way, as he grasped the steering sticks with one fleshy hand and one made of metal, it really was. Yet, even as he drove like this, Jacob could see that it was a struggle, and he could also see the worry on Whistler's face. The boy knew Brooklyn much better than the smuggler did, and it was clear that the tribesman was not as intuitive as he had once been.

They heard a bang on the side of the landship as they rolled up to the first checkpoint. Jacob popped his head through the hatch and gave the Regime's salute. He rather enjoyed saluting, but only when he did not mean it. It was a brazen two fingers up to authority without them ever actually seeing the fingers.

"Name," the checkpoint guard droned. He did not even look at Jacob, but stared at his notepad, where he had been ticking boxes all day.

"Albert Gainsley," Jacob said.

"Rank."

"Field Commander."

The guard suddenly perked up, standing straight and issuing a sloppy salute. He let his pencil drop in the process, and squinted his eyes as if it were a live grenade.

"Commander, sir."

"Pay a little more attention, lieutenant," Jacob said, doing his best impression of Rommond. "Keep dropping things and we'll drop you."

The guard gulped, and looked to his fellow guards, urging them with his eyes to let the commander through. They hauled open the gates, and Jacob dived back inside.

"I rather enjoyed that," he said.

They were waved through the next two checkpoints without issue, but at the final one they were redirected to a landing bay where other vehicles were parked. When they climbed out, they became very unsettled by the number of landships there were, and the even larger number of troops. Yet this threat had its own positive side, for, in the words of Rommond, "the larger the pile of pins, the harder it is to spot the bullet."

There was a distinct marching pattern to the troops roaming the landing bay, leading from the centre in all four directions, and rotating around the bay in a square. Jacob could not help but think that the pattern, if looked at from on high, resembled the Regime's emblem. They studied this for a moment from the viewports of the landship before hopping out and joining in. They could not afford to make a mistake. If they turned left instead of right, or kept going straight when they should have turned, it would be very obvious that they were not the battle-hardened soldiers they pretended to be.

Whistler was very worried, and he complained in the landship that he could not get the marching right. No matter how much Jacob reassured him, he was visibly nervous. Brooklyn settled into the march with ease, again relying on intuition, though having Rommond as a partner probably helped. Jacob could not help but wonder if their relationship was as disciplined as everything else. Taberah also had no problems, though Lorelai struggled with the steps. Hers could probably be forgiven, Jacob thought, given that she was wearing a medical uniform.

The troops crowded around on either side, and they moved as if they were on a conveyor belt, just another part of the factory of war. Their perfectly timed steps made the imposters all the more self-conscious, noticing every tiny error, every slight misalignment. Thankfully the troops on either side kept their faces straight ahead, and the Resistance team did likewise, though their eyes could not help but dart to the right or left to see which way they should be turning.

They had to draw the cross first, moving back into the centre, before turning to the right, but on the second turn Whistler started to rotate the wrong way, and everyone could see it from the corner of their eyes. Jacob pulled him into line, and gave him a gentle slap on the back of his head, which he tried to make look less gentle to everyone else.

"Keep up, soldier," he barked. He had seen enough barking from the dogs of war to know that this was the right thing to do.

Whistler was clearly shaken. Jacob felt bad, but he knew they would all feel a lot worse if he did not keep up the charade. They were not just in the centre of a symbol—they were in the centre of a stronghold, and no amount of dodging and ducking would save them there.

The cross was finished, and they began to form the square around it. This was easier, but they had to make that march three times, and the landing bay was huge. The team was growing tired, but fear was not just a motivator—it was fuel. As they approached the final lap, there was a sense of relief, mixed with the apprehension that the next test might not be so easy.

The troops cycled out of the area, even as new convoys and landships arrived. Jacob led his soldiers along the path leading up to the supply trains. He was surprised to find that a whole detachment of troops were following them—were following *him*. He tried not to let that surprise show. He even thought that maybe it would help. Now there were demons under his command.

Chapter Twenty-two

THE OLD TRENCH TUNNELS

Rommond and Ollie raced towards the Landquaker, diving behind the smoking ruins of landships and trucks, zig-zagging across the battlefield, even using the fires and the haze for cover. To the gunners on the Landquaker, they must have looked like scrambling ants, targets not worth firing at, but had they known it was the general out there, they would have aimed every shell in their arsenal. He was the Iron Wall of the Resistance, and they would have gladly traded theirs for him.

They were drawing close now, but Rommond dragged Ollie back behind an upturned truck.

"Not yet," he said.

He took out his spyglass and peeped over the top at the railway gun. It was very close, less than a hundred and fifty metres away, near enough that they could smell the smog. Its shortest range was one hundred metres, but it was not defenceless up close; it had many ports for sniper rifles and machine guns. Rommond did not like the idea of evading one big gun only to be downed by a smaller one. It was unbecoming.

"In around fifty metres there's a hatch," the

general explained. Despite the thick sand, he knew it was there, because the tracks had subtle markings where the entrances to the old trench tunnels were. It was a closely-guarded secret of the Resistance, one that many had died for.

"We're not going to the Landquaker?" Ollie asked, shielding his face with his scarf.

"Oh, we're going there," Rommond said, "but we're getting there from underground. Now, listen up, because this bit might get you killed. We'll have to run like the clappers for that hatch, and we'll need to dig the door out even faster. It's just inside the safe zone from the railway gun, which is why I chose this hatch instead of some of the others, but we'll be easily close enough for the snipers and the sentries."

"I can't say you're inspiring confidence." He was a young chap, a new recruit, and he needed all the encouragement he could get.

"You only need enough confidence to run," Rommond stated. "I want you scared enough to live."

Ollie's gulp was proof enough of that.

Rommond wiggled the fingers of both hands. "Get your shovels ready," he said. He waited to hear the thud and clank of the Landquaker's gun rolling into place, signalling it was about to fire. He knew it had already selected its target. If it was someone else, it bought them time to run. If it was them, then they had to run anyway. It would not be long before the next shell clicked into place.

"Run!" he cried, as the gun howled, and the howl continued in an iron reverberation.

He charged out, and Ollie followed. They galloped

across the desert, their boots carving pockets in the sand, the dust spraying up behind them. It was a sprint to the finish line, but when they crossed it, they would have another race they had to win.

As they ran, they saw the giant barrel turning in place. It was so slow, and they were so fast, and yet it seemed that they were always trying to catch up with it, before its shells caught up with them.

Rommond heard the sounds much louder now, the sharp metal cry, and the wailing echo that followed, and he felt the shudder in the ground and in his heart. He saw the blast from the gun as it pointed towards them, and knew that now they had to outrun Death as well.

"Run!" he bellowed.

No aches held him back. Though his knees stung, and his muscles throbbed, and the sweat swam into his eyes, he fired up the bellows of his body and pushed his limbs like pistons, charging ahead as fast as he had ever ran in his youth. He passed by Ollie, and wanted to reach out and drag him with him, but his momentum forbade him, and Ollie was fuelling a furnace of his own.

The blast struck behind them, only metres away, throwing them forward, but not knocking them down. The gust lashed them with sand, but it also disguised them, and what irritation it caused was nothing compared to what might have happened had they been but a second slower.

They reached where Rommond estimated the hatch was. The general halted, but Ollie kept going.

"Back here!" Rommond shouted.

Ollie skidded in place and stumbled over, before racing back to him. Rommond was already digging furiously with his hands, and Ollie dived into the sand, scooping it out by the fistful. Their fingers burned from the hot sand, which stung any little cuts or blisters they had, but they dug their way through the pain, glad they were still feeling anything at all. They could hear more sounds from the Landquaker nearby, and every noise seemed like the opening of a gun-port.

In time, Rommond found the handle of the hatch, though it was close to the edge of where they burrowed. He yanked it hard, but there was too much sand on top. They cleared away some more, but still the door would not budge. The weight of years was upon it; it was sealed by abandonment as well as sand.

Rommond caught sight of what looked like a sniper gun from the corner of his eagle eye. He dove at Ollie, knocking him to the ground, just as a bullet skipped through the sand nearby. He strained his sight to make out their attacker, then knelt down, and grabbed the rifle from his back.

"Stay down, soldier," he said to Ollie. He was saying it to the sniper as well.

He aimed, and squinted, until he thought he could see the sniper putting his reloaded rifle back in place. He knew he was in the crosshairs, but he knew the sniper was in his as well. He fired, and did not wait for confirmation of the kill. He dived back down, just in case the sniper got his final shot, but the bullet never came.

There was no time for rest. This was not a

reprieve. Even as the sniper fell, another was no doubt preparing to take his place. Or maybe it would be a machine gunner, who did not bother lining up the shot. A spray of bullets would do the trick. You could avoid a drop of rain. You could not avoid a downpour.

Rommond and Ollie cleared off more of the sand, and then struggled to pull open the hatch door. With their combined strength, it started to give way. They just needed a little more force. By now the muscle fatigue was kicking in, stealing that little more they needed to give.

"Give me your scarf," Rommond said, before snatching it from Ollie. He wrapped it around the hatch handle and used it to give him some leverage. He dug his boots into the ground and arched back, letting gravity do some of the work. Ollie joined him. Gravity worked better with more weight behind it.

The door creaked and cracked open, and the sand flooded the chamber inside. At that very moment, even as Rommond and Ollie divided inside, a hail of bullets struck the open door, piercing it like it might have pierced them. Rommond pulled the hatch closed with Ollie's scarf, and let out his much-needed sigh of relief. The bullet holes in the hatch door let in just enough light to show their heaving forms.

When the general recovered his breath, he handed Ollie back the tattered scarf. "Well, that worked in a pinch," he said. "Perhaps it should be standard military attire."

Rommond rummaged in his pocket, striking a match. He moved it around the small circular room they were in, till he found what he was looking for:

an oil lamp dangling from the wall. He grabbed it and fed its starving wick a flame.

"Tell me, Ollie," Rommond said, as he tried to open the door to the next room. "I don't really know you, so what got you into all this?"

"Yeah, I guess you don't get much time to fraternise with the troops."

"It's not because I don't want to," the general said, but the truth was that he normally did not. Out of a hundred new recruits, less than half were lucky to see their second year in the field, and less than ten percent made it to become an officer. He preferred to get to know the more seasoned troops, because they did not die so easily.

"I've got a wife," Ollie said, shaking the sand from his hair. "We wanted kids, but … well, y'know."

Rommond nodded. "The Regime's been doing the family planning for us."

"Can't wait for this war to be over," Ollie replied. "I'm hoping me and the missus will still get our chance before we're too old."

Rommond was not so optimistic. *Or before you're dead*, he thought. He had seen too many young and eager men come through his office. He had seen them in the trenches, watched as the war stole their youth and their enthusiasm, robbed them of their dreams, leaving them as husks, like the very world the demons came from.

The door finally opened, revealing a series of tunnels. The roof was makeshift, a patchwork of wooden and metal panels latched across, and held up here and there with wooden poles, which had now begun to splinter from the weight. They were not designed to support a thick blanket of sand as well.

Rommond held up the oil lamp, illuminating the way. "These tunnels used to see sunlight, back when there was no Landquaker, when that land beneath those tracks was the no man's land between our trenches and the ones Domas dug further east. We patched them over when we were forced to retreat, when the Iron Guard took the Landquaker from us. We didn't want them using these tunnels, so we buried them. This was where the war was waged for years. This was home for many." His mind said the rest: *This was also their graves.*

"Why didn't we use these in the attack today?" Ollie asked.

"Because the doors leading here are too close to the tracks," Rommond said. "You could try walking up, but you saw what the Landquaker did when we drove. Besides, we're not looking to sneak *by* the Wall. We're looking to blow it up."

Chapter Twenty-three

MAGICIAN DOWN

The Regime's landships and Moving Castles advanced at a much faster pace than the Resistance decoys. In time, both sides stopped at a safe distance from one another, though Mudro's men now thought it was not safe enough. Those brightly-painted decoys looked menacing—they were anything but.

The artillery fire came first, like little Landquakers. The sand exploded around the decoys, and a single shell struck the centre of the stage, destroying two of the wooden landships. Luckily for the Resistance, there was no crew inside. As the metal hail continued, and as the Regime began to advance once more, the Resistance crew abandoned the makeshift platoons, making for the handful of real trucks lined up further behind.

"We better get out of here," Lieutenant Byret said.

"Maybe they will chase us," Mudro pondered, puffing ceremonially on his pipe.

"You want that?" the lieutenant asked.

"If it means they're not chasing Rommond or Taberah, sure."

The Regime landships entered firing range, and blasted as they drove, while the artillery continued to devastate the wooden vehicles, sending splinters into the air. The crew were saved, and the trucks began their retreat, but even as they did, the Moving Castles charged after them.

The sleight of hand was over, and now the eyes of the enemy were on the hand, chasing it as it tried to reach for the next trick. The Regime soon realised that what they had destroyed, with so little resistance, was not Rommond's real army. Many of the landships turned back, making for Fort Landlock, which was then being overrun. The remaining forces pursued Mudro. The deception was over—now all that was left was the chase.

They pelted across the dusty dunes, trying to turn back towards Blackout, and yet knowing that even that city did not have many remaining forces to repel the Regime's armoured arsenal. The Moving Castles flanked them, forcing them to wind their way outside the line of fire, but there were too many of them, and they had speed to match their numbers.

The Resistance retreat ended. They were surrounded. It had been a brief flight, but they were now further away from the train tracks than before. If they had to go down, at least their deaths were a delay for the Regime. Right now, every second counted.

"We have to surrender," Byret said.

"It's just as well I'm not Rommond," Mudro replied, straightening up his waistcoat to make himself a little bit more presentable for the enemy. He hoped they let him smoke in his cell.

"He'd have us fight and die," the lieutenant said.

Mudro sighed, exhaling the last of the leaf. "I

think we might die anyway."

"Put your hands up," the Regime Field Commander called out. Mudro recognised him: Antyot Gallant, the prodigy of General Domas. He was all width, having spent equal time at the war table and the dinner table.

Mudro and the others abandoned their vehicles, casting their few weapons to the ground. It would not be much of a fight. Guns were not Mudro's weapon of choice.

"Quite a deception you pulled there," Gallant said.

"Why, thank you," Mudro responded with an elaborate bow.

Gallant smiled. "You might wish that I was deceiving you. But let me tell you this, *Magus*, the dungeons of the Hold are very real. When we're done with you, you'll wish you could just … disappear."

Chapter Twenty-four

DOUBLE DECEPTION

Jacob led his troops, both human and demon, and everything in between, towards the carriages waiting on the tracks. As he did, Taberah began to veer off towards one of the red carriages, the ones containing weapons and ammunition.

"This way, Lieutenant," he told her.

"I thought we—"

"No," Jacob said. "You're not here to think. You're here to work." He gestured towards a yellow carriage, where crewmen were dragging on sacks of grain.

Taberah glowered at him, but complied, getting on board.

"She's a feisty one," said the albino *maran* lieutenant whose contingent was instructed to bolster the forces under one Field Commander Gainsley. "Lieutenant Azrion Augustus," the man said, giving the Regime salute.

Jacob replied in kind. "On you go, Lieutenant."

The other troops followed, and Jacob stepped on board, placing his hands behind his back. He eyed them all up and down like Rommond might have done with his own forces, though the general would have noticed a crinkle or a crease in a uniform. Jacob noticed the anxious faces instead.

He sat down as the carriage took off. It was a small vehicle, rectangular in shape, with a domed roof, and it was very dim inside. It was not supposed to house troops, just food, but the Resistance attack on Blackout had made the Regime wary. It just had not made them wary enough.

Jacob stared at the troops that lined the food carriage, while they stared ahead blankly, trying not to look at anyone, or think of anything, all except Azrion, who was more watchful than most. A technician sat beside him, clasping a radio tightly. Jacob did not like there being a radio on board, but he liked it even less when a crackled voice spoke through it.

"Alert!" it said. "Fort Landlock under attack. Calling all reserves." The warning repeated periodically in that some monotonous tone.

Jacob knew what the attack was, but it came sooner than he expected, or perhaps their march just took far too long. He glanced outside to see a host of dust devils descending on the other carriages, and an even larger host of tribespeople standing at the top of the mountainous ridge.

"We have to go back," Azrion said. He gestured to the small window, where they could see the red carriage behind them, armed with a full contingent of soldiers, starting back towards Landlock. Jacob caught the look of haughty denial in Taberah's eyes. He was only glad that they had not boarded the trooper transport. "They need us!" Azrion added.

"No," Jacob replied. "We have our own mission."

The smuggler had gotten so used to being part

of a plot, that he could not help but think of one of his own. He had been wondering how the Resistance would get control of the Landquaker with so many extra Regime soldiers boarding with them, when he began to think that maybe they could help.

"Soldiers," he said.

The men immediately pricked their demon ears. The humans did likewise, but they were startled more. This was not in the script. Going off script was sometimes needed, but other times it got you killed.

Jacob leant in, lowering his voice. "We've gotten word of another imminent threat," he said. "There's a team of commandos plotting to attack the Iron Wall." He almost said Landquaker. The Regime did not use that name. They did not care for Rommond's rhyming monikers.

The faces of the Regime soldiers did not change a bit, while the faces of the Resistance ones were obvious—much too obvious for Jacob's taste. The Regime faced threats all the time. Plots were a daily occurrence. But this plot was one of a kind.

"My orders, which come straight from the Iron Emperor himself," Jacob said, "are to eliminate this threat, quickly and quietly. That means we must hurry, but it also means we cannot trust this mission to anyone else. Who knows who is working with them. All of you have been vetted and approved of specifically for this job."

None of the soldiers budged. They waited for Jacob to tell them to do that.

"Is that clear?" he asked.

There was a chorus of "Yes, sir!" from everyone,

human and demon included.

"Good," he said, before seizing the radio. "I'll take that. I can't have any potential leaks to the Resistance about this." He smashed it beneath his foot.

The sandy-haired technician stood up in shock. "But I'm communications," he protested. "I'm supposed to report back."

"You report to me now, soldier. What's your name?"

"Tardo Illsrid."

"Well, Tardo," Jacob replied. "You're going to be a little bit more than communications on this mission. I hope you're up to it."

I hope we all are, Jacob thought.

The journey passed in awkward silence. The gentle rocking of the carriage, and the comfort of the pliable bag behind him, might have made Jacob fall asleep, were it not for the nervous glances from his accomplices, each look etching away at his nerve.

Whistler stared at his polished boots. Perhaps he was too used to scuffed, sand-covered shoes, but Jacob knew that he was having a difficult time trying to blend in. He might have looked entirely out of place were it not for the two young cadets in Azrion's unit. Both of them were around Whistler's age, and one of them was just as much a late bloomer as he was, so much so that his cuffs covered half of his hands. There were many soldiers in the Regime forces like this. *Hell, they're not soldiers*, Jacob thought. *They're just kids*. They might have been, but they would die like soldiers all the same.

There was a sudden beep from Azrion's chronometer.

"Top-up time," he said, before taking out a small pouch of Hope. The other soldiers followed suit, taking a pinch of the powder and sprinkling it into their mouths.

Jacob suddenly realised that neither he nor the other Resistance members, except Lorelai, had a similar pouch. She took out hers, dipping her finger inside.

"Did you forget your ration?" Azrion asked.

"It's in my other uniform," Jacob said.

Azrion furrowed his brow. "Your *other* uniform?"

Jacob tried to mask his gulp. Maybe that was not the right thing to say. If he really had another uniform, it would have had Resistance emblems on it.

"That's above your grade," he said. In theory, it was. A lieutenant would not know what a commander was entitled to. For all Azrion knew, Jacob could have an entire wardrobe.

"Here, have some of mine, sir," Lorelai offered, handing him her pouch. He wished she had not, but it seemed like Azrion's intent gaze would not falter until he ingested some of the drug. "I don't want you getting sick, sir," Lorelai added.

Jacob stared into the bag. There was not a lot left, as Lorelai had not received a top-up since stumbling over to the enemy's side. But there was enough to get very intoxicated, enough to lose himself in, to forget his troubles, and forget the mission. He felt a deep-rooted urge to scoff the lot, and wished Cala had not dragged him down to her level. The problem with her level was that no matter how much it looked like the bottom, she always found a way to dig deeper.

Jacob felt everyone watching him, judging him. On one side, the Regime wanted him to take it, and on the other, so did the Resistance, all except—perhaps—Whistler, who had witnessed what Hope did to people, to human people.

He took a sprinkle, less than the others, but he tried to make it look like he took more. He rubbed his fingers together over his open mouth. He felt the tang of the powder on his tongue, and wished it could stay there, and not enter his bloodstream. He glanced at Taberah, and he thought that maybe she got the message. *If I'm not up for this*, he thought, *you'll need to take over.*

But when Lorelai took back the pouch, she handed it to the scarlet lady next. After all, *she* was supposed to be *maran* too. The sickness affected them all. It almost seemed to Jacob like Lorelai was deliberately botching the mission, but he was not sure, and already the Hope was beginning to feed his mind with suspicion and doubt.

Taberah took her hit with ease, as if she had done it many times before. She was good at pretending, at lying. The question was: could she lie her way through the symptoms? The demons did not get high—they got well. For humans, it was the opposite.

Taberah turned, and Whistler was next. He bit his lip and looked at Jacob. Everything could go terribly wrong now. They might have been able to kill the soldiers, but the secrecy of their mission would be over. They could not afford to have the eyes of the enemy upon them, and Azrion was very watchful. He was watching Whistler now.

Brooklyn snatched the bag from the boy and held it up. "Iron Plague is longer in my bones. Youth will respect their elders and let them eat first." He dipped his hand into the bag, but Azrion interrupted him.

"You, soldier," he said, "what's *your* name?"

Brooklyn sprinkled the white dust back slowly into the bag. "Rubion."

"Like Rubion the Red?" Azrion asked. "The first Birth-master?"

Brooklyn nodded slightly. "It is good name."

"Not a very common name though."

"I am not common person."

"No," Azrion said, squinting his eyes. "You're not."

Taberah looked to Jacob, and he saw that she was communicating something back. It was not words or thoughts. Her hand was inching its way to her gun.

"Your skin," Azrion said, pointing to Brooklyn. "What happened to it?"

Brooklyn shook his head. "I do not know what you mean."

"It's very *dark* skin," the lieutenant said. The emphasis betrayed his feelings well—it was almost as if the very word left a bad taste in his mouth. He moved his jaw, as if crushing each of those four letters.

"Been out in the sun too long," Jacob said. "That's mechanics for you."

"Really?" Azrion asked, his own pallid complexion standing out in stark contrast. "Not the mechanics I know. White as my hair. Pale as … what did the humans call it? Snow?"

The carriage jolted over a bump, like a body on the tracks. Everyone inside rocked a little. Everyone inside was silent a little more. Everyone inside looked at everyone else a lot.

"Well, men," Jacob said. "We have—"

"You'd almost swear," Azrion interrupted, "that you were one of those *savages* from the Wild North." His eyes bore through Brooklyn like the drills used in the iron mines. It was as if there was no one else in the carriage. Nothing else mattered but the colour of Brooklyn's skin.

Brooklyn was about to speak, perhaps even about to confess, and Taberah was about to shoot, when the carriage halted suddenly.

"What's that?" Jacob asked.

Azrion licked his lips and shook his head. "That's docking time … Commander."

They all stood up, and two of the soldiers opened the front door, just in time for them to see the front of the Landquaker before them. It was so close that they could barely see the top. Their sight was conquered by an immense grill, the so-called "cowcatcher" used to deflect objects from the tracks. It towered over them, so it must have caught some very large cows.

From there they could also hear the sound of turret fire, and the haunting echo of the railway gun's blasting barrel. Jacob hoped they would not be caught up too much in the fight.

"Seems you were right about the attack," Azrion said. "Looks like Resistance landships out there. We better get on board quick. We're sitting ducks in this supply train."

Chains were cast out, and crewmen on the railway gun pulled the supply train closer before latching it in place. Then a large ramp was lowered down, bridging the small door on the food carriage with the larger door up much higher on the railway gun. Yet it did not close the gap entirely, and a mistimed jump might have added another animal for the pilot grill to catch.

"After you," Azrion said, gesturing to Jacob.

Jacob gave the slightest of nods, even less than he should have for his rank. He felt like giving none at all, or giving the larger kind of nod that involved smashing his skull in the lieutenant's face. He wished it was the Hope that made him think that, but he knew it was not.

Jacob stepped out onto the small platform, railed on either side. There was a fairly large gap between the platform and the ramp, and Jacob did not feel like using the chains joining them as a tightrope. He leapt across, and thought that his leap was probably rather undignified for a Commander. As he reached the top of the ramp, he looked at Azrion and hoped he tripped.

But Azrion did not jump across next. He nodded to Tardo, who hopped across with ease. Then, as Jacob looked back to see who next was joining them, he felt a sudden sting on the back of his neck, before realising that Tardo had struck him there with the butt of his gun.

Chapter Twenty-five

CHANGING WEAPONS

"What happened to Rommond?" Leadman called to his commanders.

"We don't know," one of them said.

"He went down," said another.

Leadman rolled his eyes. "One hell of a time to die." He paused for a moment, then straightened up. "Right. If Rommond's gone, then I'm taking charge. This is a fool's plan, and the fool is dead. We need another."

"Another fool?" one of the commanders asked.

"Another plan!" the general snapped.

"What do you want to do?"

The explosions continued outside, and Leadman grabbed a handle on the ceiling of the landship as it rocked from the blasts.

"Forget this central push. Let's head north and regroup with the savages. Dividing our forces like this was a suicidal plan. Three weak prongs are not as good as one strong one. Let's trade in this trident for a spear."

Rommond had spent enough time in and around landships to know their subtle sounds, and he heard them turning on the spot. He raced to the nearest watchpoint, and pulled down the shutter. It had been abandoned so long that the sand had gathered thick outside, so he had to poke a hole in it with his hand. He peered out, even as one of Leadman's landships rolled straight overhead. They were heading north.

"No," Rommond said, shaking his head.

"What's wrong?" Ollie asked.

"They're leaving the battle."

Ollie sunk his head. "I guess it isn't going so well."

"They haven't even *tried*."

"Well, bravery's not for all."

"They're not fleeing, Ollie. They're regrouping, and in this case, that's worse."

"Why?"

Rommond banged the shutter closed. "Sleight of hand is no good if after the distraction, you wave the hand they did not see. We don't want more attention up north, and besides, the tribes don't need the Landquaker firing upon them. I'm sure they have enough to worry about up there."

"What can we do?"

"We find a way to catch up."

They continued on, following the winding paths, taking the trails the messengers ran in bygone days. They passed by rusted bunks, where the soldiers of old slept. The stench was terrible. Yet it was not any better when there was no roof. Rommond could remember everything too well. Once that smell set up bunk in your nostrils, it never left.

The general stopped suddenly, smacking the palm of his hand into Ollie's chest. They heard faint sounds from the room up ahead.

"So it seems they discovered these tunnels," Rommond whispered. "Let's show them what lurks beneath."

He kicked open the door, startling the guards inside, who were sitting down for tea. Two of them reached for their weapons, but the general shot them dead.

"Where are the keys?" he asked the last remaining guard, who still held his cup and saucer, though now a lot more unsteadily. "Where are the keys?" Rommond shouted.

The guard nodded to the cabinet in the corner.

"Thank you," the general said, before unloading another bullet. He could afford to waste them down here, as he knew there were spare supplies. And besides, a bullet spent on a demon was never wasted.

"God," Ollie gasped. "I'm glad I'm on your side."

Rommond rooted through the cabinet, casting a large set of keys to Ollie. "Search for the one numbered 001."

"What'll you be doing?"

Rommond grabbed the gun that was still holstered to one of the guards, and kicked the man away from it. "I'll be stocking up."

The general collected as many weapons and ammunition as he could hold or strap to his belt. He knew there were several more rooms ahead that were likely filled with guards. Ollie rummaged through the keys, cursing every now and then.

"You'd think you'd have put them in order!" he called out. A few minutes later he cried again, "Found it! No, wait. Yes!" He had the wipe away the grime to be sure.

"Good," the general said. "Come with me."

Ollie handed Rommond the key, and Rommond handed him a gun. "I hope you're not just a driver."

They continued through the tunnels, turning this way and that, finding the odd lone guard strolling through. With such a ruckus up above, the last thing they expected was to find the action down in those tunnels. For many in the Regime, it was a luxury job, laying back while others did the fighting. Not today. Today it was a curse.

Rommond halted outside the next room, where silhouettes passed back and forth.

"Listen," the general whispered. He closed his eyes for a moment. He heard several sets of footsteps, some of them moving together. It was hard to make out the number, but he listened intently until he got a decent estimate, and a more than decent idea of where the guards were standing.

"There are two at our closest right," the general told Ollie. "You take those. I'll get the rest."

Before Ollie even nodded, Rommond burst through the door, firing with guns in both hands. He took down the guard by the bookcase, bloodying the books, which were just Regime propaganda anyway, and he fired at the guard mid-stride and mid-sentence, ensuring he would never walk or talk again. Then Rommond turned to get the guard in the left corner near the door, who had an awkward to aim rifle, and turned again to get another running in from the farthest connecting corridor. By the time his eyes met with the location he had given Ollie, he saw the two guards there slumped dead.

"Better them than me," Ollie said.

Rommond slapped him on the back. "That's the spirit."

He led Ollie through the next corridor to two large sealed doors, printed with huge, faded numbers: 001.

Ollie bit his lip. "I'm hesitant to ask."

Rommond smiled. "You'll see soon enough."

He opened the lock and pulled open the doors, one at a time. It took a lot of effort, and Ollie was not much help. The metal doors scraped across the ground, and Rommond grimaced from the screeching steel. It was pitch black inside, which made Ollie shudder. It could have been anything in there. A machine. A monster. Maybe nothing at all.

"What are we looking for?" Ollie asked.

The general held up the oil lamp. Inside they saw the silhouette of an old landship, covered in cobwebs.

Rommond smiled. "A bigger gun."

Chapter Twenty-six

ON THE EDGE

As Taberah saw Jacob go down, her gun went up. She knew she could not kill all of the Regime soldiers in time, but she was not going down without a fight. If she fell, at least some of the demons would too. Azrion would be one of them.

The lieutenant already had his hands up. "Woah!" he cried. "I'm on your side!"

Little did he know. The problem was, Taberah was not so sure that he did not.

"Put that away, soldier," Azrion ordered.

"I'll put it in your head," Taberah hissed.

"You've got some nerve talking to a lieutenant like that."

"You've got some nerve taking out a commander like that," she replied, nodding to Jacob's slumped form across the way.

"I had nothing to do with that, I assure you."

"That soldier you sent across. Is he not one of your men?"

"He is, but—"

"Then take some responsibility, *Lieutenant*."

Azrion clenched his fists, but said nothing.

"We should be calm," Brooklyn urged.

"Stay out of this, soldier," Azrion replied.

Taberah clicked the safety off. "What was with all the questions back there?"

"What, with him?" Azrion asked, gesturing to Brooklyn. "With ... *Rubion*?"

"Yes."

"It's just procedure," he said. "You can't be too careful,"

"No," Taberah replied, keeping the gun steady. "No, you can't."

"I hate to interrupt a good verbal lashing," Lorelai said, "but I need to go across to tend to the Commander."

"You're not going anywhere," Taberah replied.

"You can shoot me if you want," Lorelai said, "but if you really care about your commander, you won't stop me." She marched off, bracing herself. She clearly expected Taberah to reply with gunfire.

"I should have one of my men over there," Azrion said. "In case that nurse isn't on our side."

Taberah glared at him. "You already have a man over there."

"I keep telling you ... I didn't order that attack!"

Taberah looked at Brooklyn and Whistler. "You two, join the nurse."

They complied, hopping across to the other side, where they found Jacob in Lorelai's arms, mumbling away to himself.

"That was a nasty whack he got there," the nurse said. "He's coming to now."

They expected to see Taberah jump across next,

but they heard a commotion in the food carriage, and saw Azrion's soldiers diving on her, before he slammed the carriage door shut. There was gunfire, and shouts and screams, then hushed voices, followed by silence, as if sound was swiftly dying.

"Oh no, what do we do now?" Whistler asked.

"Keep to the mission," Lorelai said.

The door in the other carriage opened again, and they could see Taberah tied up. All things considered, that was not too bad. They expected to see her dead.

Azrion jumped across and crouched down with the others.

"How's he doing?"

Jacob opened his eyes now. "Who's that? Is that you, dad?"

"He's coming around," Lorelai said. "Just give him a minute." She rubbed her hand across his forehead.

"Wish I had a nurse like you when I was in the trenches," Azrion said with a grin.

She forced a smile.

"What's your name?" he asked her. "I think I might request you in my unit."

"Oh, I don't think the Commander would allow it."

"I'm going for a promotion soon," he replied. "I just need a few more kills."

He looked about, as if he might make them then and there.

"I asked you your name," he said.

Only Jacob and Taberah had prepared names, and had the credentials to back them up. The lower ranks did not carry identification, largely because they died quicker than the clerks could issue them. The team expected Jacob to do most of the talking. He could not do much of that in his current state.

"Elizah," Lorelai said in time. "Elizah Botherford."

Whistler made a squeak, and Azrion glared at him. "What is it?"

"Oh, I, uh, I … what happened over there?" Whistler stuttered.

"Don't you worry about that, cadet. We neutralised the threat. I think she might have been working with Tardo. The turncoat! I always suspected he had Resistance sympathies. He can sympathise with them for a long time in the Hold … providing I don't kill him first."

He looked back at the food carriage, where the other soldiers were hauling Taberah across. She struggled in her bonds, and she might have screamed and shouted too, were she not gagged. They dropped her with a thud on the ramp, and she rolled down a little, dangling dangerously close to the edge. From there she had the perfect vantage point to watch the food carriage's wheels rotate, before it moved sideways off the track, clearing the way for the Landquaker to advance forward.

The soldiers dragged Taberah up and carried her through the corridor.

"We'll find out what she knows," Azrion said. He paused for a moment, rubbing his chin. "You know, she looks a little familiar. I wonder where I've seen her before."

On a Wanted poster, Jacob thought. He was fully awake now, and had come to his senses. It was a good thing that Whistler had tucked his hair into his military cap or Azrion might have noticed the resemblance. One scarlet strand slipped out behind his ear, a little turncoat of its own.

They helped Jacob to his feet, and he placed his cap back on.

"I want to know who hit me," he said.

"That'd be Turncoat Tardo," Azrion said.

"With a name like that, you'd think he'd be better watched," Jacob quipped.

"I'll get him for you, Commander, don't you worry. Maybe if I do, you can repay me by transferring Elizah over to my unit." He winked at her, and she grimaced. He took out his revolver, span the barrel, and snapped it back into place. "Time to hunt some traitors."

He marched off, and Brooklyn and Whistler followed slowly. Taberah was already well out of sight. When they were all out of earshot, Jacob looked at Lorelai and asked, "Elizah?"

"I improvised."

"You couldn't think of a better name?"

"It's a nice name."

"Yeah," Jacob said, "it's a nice name for the dead."

Chapter Twenty-seven

ALL ABOARD

Ollie helped clear away the cobwebs, but he could not clear away the rust. It looked very old, a hunk of junk to anyone else's eyes, but to Rommond it seemed like a treasure. Not a treasure that glints on the exterior, but shines in the heart.

"It doesn't have a name or number," Ollie called from behind the vehicle.

"Oh, it does," the general replied. "The nameplate is back in Blackout. I have it hanging on my wall. This, my friend, is the first, the prototype, the quintessential. This is Brooklyn."

They climbed in, and Rommond oiled up the controls, while Ollie dragged several bags of coal aboard. The tunnels might have been abandoned, but there were still plenty of supplies there. Ollie just wished it included newer landships.

When the engine roared to life, the vessel hummed, and the noise made it sound more than a little frightening. Ollie imagined what it must have been like those early years in the trenches, when this surprise monster rolled across them, announcing the dawn of machine warfare. As Rommond grabbed

191

the steering sticks, it seemed the world was about to relive those terrifying days.

The general drove the landship forward slowly, turning it even slower, until he faced one of the ramps leading to the boarded-up ceiling. Ollie had not thought much of those ramps, but it was their ticket to freedom. They had to get out quick, because the train was leaving. There was no last call of "all aboard."

The landship burst through the ceiling of the tunnels, emerging into the onslaught of the sun. The land around was burnt by more than just its sniper rays. Smoke rose in pillars from all the metal wounds, and where there was not metal, there was black sand smothering the yellows and smouldering the reds.

Rommond saw the Landquaker heading north, where everyone was converging, the meeting place of many guns. He followed it, racing across the track, wishing his landship was the Hopebreaker, wishing it ran on diesel instead of steam. He knew that if the Landquaker sped ahead, he could not match its speed, but he also knew that it had to slow down some time, that when the tracks ran out, it had to stop completely. He just hoped it would not take that long, because by then the team upon the railway gun might be dead.

"I can't shovel this coal fast enough," Ollie said.

"Do you want to drive instead?" Rommond called back, irritated.

"I don't think I can drive this thing as fast as you."

"Then feed that furnace as if it were the mouth of Hell," the general said.

The heat inside the landship grew by the minute. Everything was burning in its own way. While the fires lapped at Ollie's hands, Rommond was burning rubber, trying to get that little extra speed.

Out of the view-port, the general saw a large bend in the rails up ahead, the turn in the track, the corner of the Iron Wall. Instead of following it directly, as the Landquaker had to, slowing down to take that turn, he drove off the tracks and cut across the gravel. Rommond was not the guy to cut corners in most other areas of life, but here it was a lifesaver. He just hoped it was as much a lifesaver for the others as it was for him.

Yet the Regime had more than the Landquaker on those rails. A small steam-pod chugged along the tracks, spotting Rommond's rust bucket. The crew fired token shots towards the landship, less of an attempt to pierce the hull and more of an announcement that they were there, that they would be as dogged in the hunt as he was in his pursuit of the railway gun. Together they formed a train of a different kind, of mismatching carriages, separated from each other, and yet united in the chase.

The pods were a nuisance, a distraction, riling up Rommond's own nuisance and distraction: Ollie. He frequently abandoned his shovelling to glance out of the viewports, yelling about their pursuers. "They're gaining on us!" he cried.

"Not for long," the general called back, before halting the landship and turning it sharply. A rattle of gunfire pierced the spot where it had been, but Rommond was already driving it back in an arc.

"That's the wrong direction!" Ollie shouted.

"Not for this," Rommond said. "Hold on tight."

Ollie glanced out again, just in time to see the side of the steam-pod before Rommond crashed the landship into it, knocking it off the track, where it landed on its side in a plume of sand.

"Now," the general said. "Get back to shovelling."

Ollie picked himself up and resumed his duties, while Rommond returned to the chase, following the track again, glad that his head-on collision had just dented the front of the landship, and bent the turret. He was not going to use it anyway. He needed speed, not shells.

In time he saw the Landquaker ahead, thundering down the track. He was catching up. He could already smell the smoke the railway gun spewed. It smelled fouler than it was when in Resistance hands, almost as if it had been contaminated with the Iron Plague.

As he drove closer, the train grew larger, dwarfing the landship. It was not so much a game of cat and mouse, but mouse and cat. At any moment the tables could turn. That gigantic turret could turn. But there was a benefit in being small, in going unnoticed.

But he did not go unnoticed. Several steam-pods were in pursuit, gaining on him even as he gained on the Landquaker. The tracks spat out sparks in protest as every driver pushed their vehicle beyond its limits, as if Death were chasing them. In many ways, he was. His name was Edward Rommond.

Gunfire began to litter the hull of the landship. Ollie jumped and yelped, and he even blocked the rear viewport with his shovel. The bullets pierced the metal, letting in little beams of light, like spotlights for the snipers.

"We won't make it!" Ollie screamed, cowering now behind the gunner's seat. More daylight streamed in, pointing its golden fingers at him.

"The landship mightn't make it," Rommond said, ducking from a bullet that ricocheted inside. He did not like the irony that he might die to a trademark trickshot. He would rather face his dying bullet, not take it in the back.

"We'll have to surrender," Ollie suggested.

Rommond scoffed at the notion. It was not a word in his dictionary. But it did exist in his old book of tactics, where the white flag was offered just long enough to turn the enemy's one red. He knew it would not work now. They had grown wise to his ways. But he had many ways, and they were not wise to them all.

The landship was slowing down, but the gap between it and the Landquaker was small.

"Rommond, this piece of junk won't get us there!" Ollie cried.

"We only need it to get us so far."

Rommond jammed the steering sticks forward, locking them in place, letting it chug along as if it had a mind of its own. He got up, dodging another bullet. The daylight continued to puncture the walls, highlighting the escape hatch at the bottom of the vehicle. Rommond kicked the hatch door open, hearing it clang on the metal tracks below.

"What are you doing?" Ollie called.

"Escaping."

"Are you mad? We're still moving."

"So are they."

"You'll never roll out of the way in time."

"I don't want to roll *out* of the way," Rommond replied. "I want to roll *under*."

He lowered his feet out of the hatch, tucking them under the floor of the landship. There was not a lot of space there, so he had to tuck them in tight. He held onto the edge of the hatch with his elbows. He had to time his drop just right. If he did it too early, and did not duck in time, he could lose his head in the process, or be dragged across the tracks like a rag doll.

The moment came, and he let go, straightening up as he fell onto the track. He felt the rush of air pass him, and he turned his head to the side, feeling the heat of the landship blowing by his ear. Then daylight assaulted his eyes, and he squinted against the glare. He had to time the next bit even better, and he would not have the benefit of sight to help him.

He shimmied until he got his arms up tight against his chest. He knew there was a bar beneath the steam-pod, just like there was beneath most landships, there to help the engineers pull themselves under when doing repairs. It was close enough to the hatch. *Close enough* was all he needed.

The sun blotted out, and Rommond knew that the steam-pod was passing overhead. He reached out, and his fingers felt the metal of the vessel's floor. Then they felt the bar, and he grabbed on tight. It did not take even a second to pull him violently across the track. The notches in the rails battered his back and legs. He tucked his head up to avoid them knocking him out as well. He groaned and cried as the track assailed him, but the pain only fuelled his strength. He used all of it to pull himself up close to the steam-pod's floor, away from that awful torture rack beneath. It was a struggle to hold on, and an even great struggle to hold his entire weight up like this. He felt some metal plating jutting out of the bottom of the vehicle near his feet, so he pressed his boots against it, which relieved some of the pressure, but then his boots slipped against the metal, and his leg struck the track again. His uniform was torn. His skin was torn. But his will was unbroken.

He bashed his fist against the hatch, slipping as he did so, and hauling himself back up just as quick. Nothing happened. He struck it again, with much more force, until it rattled on its hinges. He could hear the crew inside moving about, drawing closer, mumbling something to each other. It sounded like mumbles, but it smelt a lot like fear. The hatch opened, and there was the face of a very perplexed Regime soldier. Rommond grabbed his gun and fired quick, too quick for the soldier to jump away. His blood stained the general's uniform. It did not matter. He needed a new one anyway.

The other guards did not appear at the opening. It was not wisdom that held them back. It was terror. The smell was more palpable now with the hatch open, but then the interior of all landships smelt just as bad. The enemy would not come to Rommond, so he had to send his bullets out looking for them. He fired three shots into the hatch at an angle, aimed in three different directions, all the while struggling to keep his grip, to keep his feet pressed against the metal ridge. He heard the shouts of the people inside, and then he heard the ricochet of the bullets, and then he heard nothing at all.

His strength finally gave way. He could not haul himself inside. His feet slipped, and his hands followed. He struck the track with a thud, and the steam-pod rolled over him, revealing the waiting sun, with its vendetta against his eyes. The pain was worse now, a mix of sharp and stabbing, and gnawing aches. His muscles were strained, and his eyes were squinted, but he knew he had to get up and look around, and run, and fight, and not let the Landquaker get away.

He hauled himself up, even as the pain tried desperately to pin him down. He gritted his teeth, roaring through the tiny gaps in them as he stumbled forward towards the slowing steam-pod with its skeleton crew. He pulled the door open and threw himself inside, grabbing his gun just in case. But they were all dead, or dying fast enough that they did not deserve another bullet. There were many more on the Landquaker more deserving.

He fired the vehicle up, and set it to full speed. It had an automated system for filling the furnace that just needed a few cranks every now and then to keep it going. It was the kind of thing that Brooklyn might have invented, had he not lost his spirit connection. Cogs sent a series of pipes up and down, and coal rolled out. Rommond preferred the reliability of good old-fashioned manpower, but it was only reliable if it was there. Those three dead soldiers clearly were not reliable enough.

As he sat in the driver's seat, watching the Landquaker from the viewport, and watching the battered landship in front of him, he felt the pain grow. He had the time now to focus on it, to look at his wounds. He could feel the warm wetness of the blood upon his back, and he could feel it drop down his legs. He could also feel the deeper bruising where the tracks had riddled him with iron punches.

In time the Landquaker halted, and Rommond was not sure why. The landship in front caught up, gently ramming the iron beast before it, and Rommond's steam-pod followed suit, ramming the landship in turn. He struggled out, kicking the arms of the Regime guards as he passed, growling through the pain.

He stumbled over to the landship and banged on the hull. There was no response. He peered through one of the many bullet holes, and sighed as he saw Ollie's bloodied body curled up on the floor.

Then he saw why the Landquaker had stopped. On the horizon there were many little figures, black against the sun. They were advancing quickly, like a stampeding herd, so quick that Rommond could soon make out what they were: a gang of men and women in black leather upon large diesel-powered bikes. Then he heard a series of loud clangs and clicks, and he knew just what they signalled. A large shadow passed over him. The railway gun was swivelling around to face the many tiny guns that now approached.

Chapter Twenty-eight

TRACKING TRAITORS

Jacob and his team searched for Tardo, Azrion leading the charge, though really the smuggler was hoping to find Taberah instead. The plan was unravelling, yet she was tied up tight. He only hoped they were not torturing her, or worse.

Many of the rooms they searched were empty, filled only with supplies. It was better than being filled with soldiers. Jacob did not need more demon troops under his command.

"Wait till I find him," Azrion said, raising a clenched fist. "Never trusted him. Never trusted comms in general." He turned sharply, grabbing Jacob's shoulder. "It's just as well you broke his radio."

"Indeed," Jacob said, glancing at Lorelai.

It might have been the Hope, but Jacob found himself staring at the back of Azrion's frosted hair, and contemplating whacking him with his gun. That was not part of the plan either, but it sounded like a good addition.

They opened another door, and jumped back when they found Taberah there, sitting down on a chair, arms folded. The soldiers who had tied her up lay dead upon the ground, strangled by the ropes that previously bound her. They had not tied them tight enough.

"Finally," she said. She was a little bruised, her fiery hair plunging out of her cap. She looked a lot more like the leader of the Order then, and the image in the Wanted posters.

"You!" Azrion cried.

"Just me," she replied. "Next time don't leave children to restrain me."

Azrion raised his gun. "There's another prison you can't escape from."

Jacob pointed his own at Azrion. "Put it down, Lieutenant. I can vouch for her."

"She's in on it with Tardo!" Azrion protested.

"Trust me," Jacob said, "she's not."

Azrion turned to Lorelai, as if he could sense the demon in her. "What do you think, Elizah?"

Taberah's eyes lit up, and she might as well have been ablaze, for a rage burned through her, and she leapt at Azrion, knocking him to the ground. His gun went off, but it fired into the ceiling, and she knocked the gun away. Her hands flayed, and her hair flayed with them. She bashed and clawed at him. "You don't get to say that name!" she roared. "You don't get to say it!"

Jacob tried to drag her off, but she pushed him back into Lorelai. She kept bashing Azrion until her knuckles were bruised and bloodied, and his face was worse. At any other time he might have overpowered her, but years of sorrow gave her strength, and she used it all on him, as if he was singly responsible for it all. As she broke his nose and bloodied his eyes, she saw Domas in his features, and crushed them even more.

"Help me," he called out weakly to Jacob.

"Sorry, mate," Jacob replied, "but I warned you that there were Resistance commandos on board."

In time, he had to pull Taberah off the bludgeoned lieutenant, but by that time he was already dead. Her hands were covered in blood, and it was impossible to tell which was hers. The reality was that most of it was his.

"Are you okay?" Jacob asked, helping her to her feet. He handed her his handkerchief to wipe her hands clean.

"I am now."

"Maybe that was … a little overkill."

"For these demons, Jacob," she said, glancing at Lorelai, "that's just what they need."

They continued on, catching up with Brooklyn and Whistler, who were strolling through the corridor. With no more Regime soldiers under his command, Jacob was finally able to focus on the real mission: finding the control room, and wrestling back control of the railway gun.

They searched several more rooms, a few empty, a few others housing soldiers priming weapons for the gun ports. To these Jacob made a vague, unobjectionable command, and gave the now familiar salute. The soldiers were so focused on the battle, they did not realise it waged inside as well.

The next room the team searched was not empty. They found someone hiding behind several barrels.

"Stay back!" Tardo shouted, firing a token shot in their direction.

"Stand down, soldier," Jacob called out.

"Long live the Resistance!" Tardo cried.

Jacob laughed. "You know, we're actually on your side."

He dodged another bullet. *Maybe not.*

"You can kill us, but more will take up the banner!" the soldier yelled. He sounded like a new recruit. Resistance veterans just were not that enthusiastic.

"Hell, Tardo, we *are* the Resistance!" Jacob shouted back.

There was silence for a moment, and then Tardo peeked out. "You are?"

"I'd try to prove it to you, but I'm currently … you know, undercover."

"Well … uh … what's the password?"

"There's no password, idiot," Taberah replied.

"Right. Just checking."

"Look, Tardo, we're trying to take back this thing," Jacob said.

"Landquaker," Brooklyn said.

Saying that name helped. Few in the Regime would utter it, as if the very name might make the Iron Wall crumble.

Tardo came out slowly and approached even slower.

"We're the commandos I was talking about," Jacob explained.

Tardo's face lit up. He pointed at Taberah, his hand shaking. "You're the Scorpion!" He looked at Jacob. "I don't really know who you are. I expected

Rommond to have a moustache."

"I shaved it off," Jacob said.

"Really?" Tardo exclaimed, his eyes widening.

"No," Jacob said. "I'm not really anybody, Tardo, but if you have to put me on a Wanted poster, you can call me Spider."

Tardo bit his lip. "Sorry about … hitting you back there."

"Join us and we'll call it even."

Tardo gave the Resistance salute.

"Yeah," Jacob said with hesitation. "Probably better to stick to the other one in here."

"Oh!" Tardo said. "Y-y-yes! Of course!"

"We need to keep moving," Taberah urged.

Tardo's excitement was palpable. "Oh, I heard you were *full steam ahead*!"

She glared at him.

"Maybe you can help us," Whistler suggested.

"We're trying to find the control room," Jacob added.

Tardo shook his head. "You won't get in there."

"We have to."

"Don't worry," Taberah said, holding up a small canister of thermite that she had strapped to her belt. It could burn through almost anything. "We brought our own key."

"It's not opening the door I'd be worried about," Tardo said. "It's the Conductor."

Chapter Twenty-nine

THE CONDUCTOR

The length of the Landquaker was patrolled by the elite of the elite, a masterpiece of the Iron Guard. They called it the Conductor, and it was more machine than any of its kindred, having undergone many transformations at the hands of the Regime's mechanics and surgeons. It was one and a half times the height of an average man, its spine elongated, its ribs replaced with metal plating, its skull an iron helm, its eyes mere openings into a furnace, so that when it stared at someone, they only saw fire. There was so little left of the man beneath, and people were not entirely sure if it was just one man that was the basis for this creation, or if the parts of many were used, swapped out like cogs in a machine.

The Conductor walked through the isle of the train, turning its head from side to side as it passed by the cabins, creating a metal rhythm as its iron feet struck the ground. Its back was hunched, and its legs were arched, suggesting a kind of stalking motion as it walked. Its arms swung like pendulums, and its hands were formed into eternal mechanical claws, ready at any moment to seize those who should not be on board.

Rommond had warned Jacob's team about this threat. Normal soldiers might fall for their disguise, but the general knew that the Iron Guard would not. Their memory was enhanced, to help them more easily identify their targets, but in the Conductor's case, it helped it remember who was a genuine soldier, and who was an imposter. Jacob could not just walk by. He had smuggled his team on, but he would have to smuggle them through as well.

They had to get to the control room, which was close to the centre of the vehicle. They were slightly closer to it on this side of the Landquaker, but that meant nothing when the Conductor was in their way.

"I'm kind of wishing I had one of Rommond's fancy guns right now," Jacob said.

"They'd be no good against the Conductor," Taberah replied. "He's the toughest of the lot."

"Kind of wish Soasa was here then."

Taberah let out a tiny sigh. "So do I. But for now, I'll have to do."

Jacob smiled. "I'm sure you're more than enough."

They continued on slowly, averting their gaze when troops marched past, and doing a little forced marching of their own. Every cabin now seemed occupied, and they dared not search them, knowing they might find the barrel of a gun.

Tardo led them forward, telling them how close they were getting to the control room, yet constantly reminding them that they would not make it. Even the Regime crew feared the Conductor, and did not stand in the way of its patrols.

Then they felt it. There was a shudder in the grating below their feet, a rattle of any metal not fitted tightly enough. They heard the reverberating footsteps of the Conductor approaching, and it seemed like it was treading on their hearts. Panic swept through them, as if it were an ally of the Iron Guard. It struck Tardo most of all, and he trembled where he stood.

"Quick, we need to hide," Jacob said.

They ran in all directions, pulling at doors, racing back down the way they had come. At first, it looked like some of them were running together, but when Whistler found himself in someone's bed-chamber, he found himself there alone. *Almost* alone. There was sleeping passenger behind him, whose loud snores were only slightly reassuring.

Whistler held his breath as the giant silhouette of the Conductor passed slowly by. It was such a daunting shape, a monstrous form, that it seemed to seep into the room. At the very least, it stayed in Whistler's mind.

Jacob rushed into the next room, closing the door quickly, and panting out a sigh. He turned to find three commanders hunched over a table with a map of the battlefield. One was frozen mid-pointing, while the others looked at Jacob in surprise.

The smuggler immediately straightened up and marched to the table. "Sorry I'm late," he said. "There were … pressing matters to attend to. Now, where were we?"

"Who *are* you?"

"Gainsley. Albert Gainsley."

One of the commanders furrowed his brow. "Isn't he dead?"

Jacob could see the realisation in their eyes, and their shifting hands reaching for their guns. He dived at them, knocking one of them to the ground, barely evading the bullet fired by another. He rolled around just in time for the commander on top of him to receive the second bullet. He struggled up, even as the first commander was reloading, only to be seized by the second and thrown across the room, where he whacked against a chest of drawers, which broke apart behind him. He scrambled up, grabbing a splintered plank and knocking out the armed commander. The other one charged at him, pressing him into the wall, where he left a mark. They tossed and turned with each other, pushing back and forth, breaking almost every piece of furniture in the room. The walls were imprinted with the highlights of the fight. Then, when the final commander had Jacob pinned to the floor, lying upon the tattered battle map, Jacob reached out around him, trying to grab anything, until he found a glass paperweight, which he promptly smacked the man in the skull with. He fell, dripping blood upon the miniature battlefield.

Jacob pushed the commander off of him and struggled up. He looked a lot more dishevelled now, not befitting of someone of his rank. *More like my old self*, he thought, as he gathered his breath.

He thought he better get out of there. The uniform did not amount to much if he was caught standing in a pile of commander blood. He wondered what happened to the others, if they had made it away in time, or if the Conductor had made them pay the highest fare of all.

Chapter Thirty

GHOST TRAIN

In her retreat from the Conductor, Taberah also found herself alone. She was not sure exactly where she was on the Landquaker. The interior was bland, and it looked like the walls had been stripped bare. The corridor and the rooms all looked the same. This was Rommond's baby, not hers.

The lights seemed a bit darker in this part of the carriage. The oil lamps were low. She could no longer hear the shudder of the Conductor's footfalls, but she did not fancy turning back. She thought Rommond must have had some ventilation shafts installed somewhere. Maybe she could find her way around.

She stopped in her tracks. She thought she saw something out of the corner of her eye. She thought it looked small, and a little bit like her. She thought it looked a lot like a little girl.

She turned quickly, but it was gone. Perhaps it was never there to begin with. But there was a different feeling in the carriage, the kind of feeling she had many years before, when she was chasing ghosts throughout Altadas.

"Elizah?" she called out, her voice quivering.

There was no answer.

She pressed forward, slowly, her boots sounding louder against the floor than they did previously. Every sight and sound was accentuated, as if it had to be to see those subtle sights and hear those barely audible sounds that came from the spirit world.

Then she saw her, a little girl, maybe five or six, her fiery red locks tumbling down her shoulders. She had pudgy cheeks, just a little of the baby left in her, and she had a smile, the kind of smile Taberah saw in her dreams.

Taberah fell to her knees. "Elizah," she whispered.

The girl approached, and the lights flickered as she walked. It seemed like she was walking too slow and too fast all at the same time. Maybe in the spirit world, there was no time.

"I failed you," Taberah said.

Elizah placed her tiny hand on her mother's cheek. "You didn't fail me, mommy."

"I tried to save you," Taberah sobbed. "I tried to bring you back."

"You can't do that," the girl replied.

"I know, but I tried, and I keep thinking maybe if I tried harder, if I fought harder—"

"Fight for the other ones," Elizah said.

"The other ones?"

"The other children, the other little lights they make go out."

"What can I do?" Taberah begged. "Tell me what to do."

"Find the ones who cut the cords."

"The Birth-masters?"

"Do to them what they did to us."

Taberah paused, looking at her hands, which looked a little redder than they did before. "Kill them?" she asked.

"Everyone has a mission," Elizah said. "This one is yours."

The lights flickered again, and the girl was gone.

Chapter Thirty-one

STAMPEDE OF THE OXEN

The biker gang drove furiously through the sand, and the sound of their diesel engines preceded them. They drove in formation, with their leader, Lokk, at the front, and Ana Alakovi next in line, their steel and leather chaps guarding their legs against the sand and the desert shrubs. They were grim men and women, the finest of the Oxen clan, but there were also several of the Copper Vixens, two women per bike, one driving, one brandishing a four-barrel shotgun.

Alakovi was a big woman, tall and broad, with bulging arms and hands, but the bike she rode was bigger. It was made for the biggest and the best. She revved the engine as she drove, her rainbow-streaked hair flailing in the wind, her face grimmer than it ever was before. It bore several fresh scars, as if she had more than earned her new ride. It was a black bike, with silver between the chassis. They all were. Black was the colour of the Oxen clan. It was the colour of their bikes, and it was the colour of their leather. A wave of black rolled across the yellow sands.

As the gang drew close, ports on the side of the Landquaker opened, and Regime soldiers pushed through machine guns. They began firing, but so did the bikers. Lokk took out the first gun, and all its gunners, with the first of his shotgun shells. The casing span into the desert behind, and Lokk loaded the next shell with a flick of the gun, keeping one hand firmly on the handlebar of the bike, and both eyes on the next port that opened up.

The riders split in several directions, Lokk heading towards the front, Alakovi heading towards the rear. The Regime gunners spat bullets by the dozen, taking down several bikers as they passed.

Bullets struck everywhere around the railway gun. Windows shattered, and people inside ducked and cowered. The giant barrel of the Landquaker could not reach the tiny gnats that roamed about it, but there were many other barrels locking into place.

Alakovi saw a port open near her, but she knew she could not shoot in time. She prepared to duck, knowing she was not an easy target to miss, and at the moment when she expected the click, she heard a commotion inside the railway gun. With a glance back she saw the machine gun hauled back inside, and she thought she heard Taberah's voice. What irony that it should be her that saved the Copper Matron.

Rommond had barely crawled aboard the Landquaker when he was forced to evade the watchful gaze of the Conductor. The general dripped blood like breadcrumbs, so he knew that he was not so much hiding as fleeing. He just had to flee in the right direction.

He knew the railway gun better than anyone, and found his way quickly through several passages that led to a hatch in the ceiling, which in turn led up to the roof of the vessel. He felt like he had been opening far too many hatches that day, but he knew that this was a quicker way to get to the control room. He could slip or fall, and it was a long enough way down, but at least he would not have to worry about the Conductor up there.

He was wrong.

As he hauled himself up, he heard the metal footsteps of that machine man drawing closer. The fear gave him new strength, and he clambered through the hatch all the quicker, and tried to get the door back on in time. Then he saw the top of the Conductor's gleaming head, and he froze, trying not to move or cast a shadow. Then a drop of blood betrayed him and leapt from his wounds, landing on the iron skull. The Conductor looked up, and the fire blazed brighter in his eyes.

Rommond knew he had to run. He threw the hatch door away, where it almost struck one of the bikers below, and he hobbled up the ramp leading to the main roof. Even as he moved, he could hear the sound of metal fingers on the ladder behind him, the kind of metal fingers that might soon be around his neck.

He raced on, his legs joining the conspiracy against him. In his mind, he was running. In his body, he was barely even limping along. At this rate he knew he would not make it. But if he got the Conductor out of the main hallway, he could at least buy the others some time, if they were even still alive. He wished somehow that someone could buy some for him.

As the Conductor crawled out onto the roof, several of the bikers started firing shots at it from the ground. They were not diamond-tipped bullets, but it was a welcome distraction. It was just a pity the Conductor was mostly machine, because it did not distract so easily. Its eyes were firmly planted on Rommond. It remembered his face. It remembered his number on the target list. 001.

The general trudged on, his breathing laboured, the pains in his body holding him back. He fired a token shot behind him, not stopping to take aim. He heard it clang off the metal casing that surrounded the Conductor's torso, and knew that soon he would feel the breaking of his own.

On the ground, Lokk saw the Conductor leap onto Rommond. He barely knew the man, but he knew his mission, and he knew why Alakovi had come to him. If the general died, the Resistance would lose its focus, and the Regime would refocus to take down the next in line. It would not take them long to get to Ana, or get to him.

Lokk revved his engine, and drove straight towards the Landquaker. To anyone watching, it looked like suicide. They might have thought he was trying to crash into the railway gun and ignite his engine. They might have thought he had given up hope, or was trying to hide from the Conductor in the shadow of the train. Instead, he leant back, and the front wheel came off the ground. He drove on one wheel, the front one rising higher by the second. When he was close enough to the railway gun, he pressed a button on the handlebars, which sent a grappling hook up to the top of the vehicle. It locked into place, and the spring force pulled the bike up into the air, right onto the roof of the Landquaker, right into the body of the Conductor hunched over Rommond, knocking it off the other side, where it sent up a plume of sand like a mushroom cloud.

Lokk reached down and offered his hand to the general. "Where you headin'?" he asked with a voice as thick as thunder, as if he guzzled down diesel as well as beer.

"Halfway up," Rommond said, clambering onto the back of the bike. "The control room's there."

"Hold on," Lokk replied.

They sped across the roof, skidding momentarily as the Landquaker started to move again, as the vessel rocked and rattled on the tracks. The sound of the bike must have alerted the soldiers inside, for here and there hatches opened, and soldiers popped up with guns at the ready. Lokk fired his shotgun at them, and Rommond took a second one from a cradle at the back, unloading a round at the next fool to inspect the noises on the roof.

Rommond could see Nox's signature on the handle of the gun. It did not need it. The whole design had the Coilhunter written all over it. "I've got to get one of these," he said, patting the barrel.

Lokk smiled through his thick black beard. "You just did."

Another guard cast open the hatch door ahead of them, and Lokk jumped the bike right over the cowering man's head. Rommond clung on with one hand, while firing a shell with the other. He had lost a lot of blood, but he had not lost his aim.

They continued across the roof, halting when Rommond indicated they were near the control room. Boy was he glad he did not have to hobble the entire way. He was even happier that the Conductor was not chasing him for his ticket.

"Here," Lokk said, casting Rommond a box of shells. "You'll need these. Nox is good, but he hasn't quite gone full revolver on these yet, so you run out quick."

"Thanks," the general said, tipping his cap.

"Don't thank me," Lokk replied. "I'm only here 'cause of Ana. We do our own thing, the Oxen, but today we're doin' the same as you, tearin' down the Iron Wall."

Chapter Thirty-two

QUAKE

Rommond lowered himself down the hatch, listening carefully for the sound of troops. It was very quiet, a lot quieter than he expected. It was more unsettling than the sounds of war, because he knew the war still raged around him. He could not help but fear that it was the quiet before a quake.

He peered around corners, finding his way back into the main corridor, with not a soul in sight. He found he had to use the shotgun for support. The fatigue was really kicking in. Yet he was so close to the control room now. He could feel the heat of the furnaces.

He turned another few corners, and found Brooklyn there.

"Come on, Brooklyn," he said, hobbling on. "Let's finish this."

Perhaps he should have been paying more attention. There was something off about Brooklyn, something different.

Rommond walked on, and Brooklyn followed. They reached the control room, which was sealed tight. The door was thick. Bullets could not pierce it. Even sound could not get through. Rommond placed his shotgun on the floor, groaning as he bent down, and then took his canister of thermite from his belt. He got ready to break the seal.

"I'm glad I have you with me for this," he said, though he did not turn around, and therefore did not see the blank expression on Brooklyn's face. "This is the end of the road."

He grabbed the lid of the canister and prepared to turn it open. Then he felt something at the back of his head. He knew it well enough to know that it was a gun, and he knew guns well enough to know that it was the pistol he had given Brooklyn.

He sighed and closed his eyes.

"Think about this, Brooklyn. This isn't you."

It did not matter who it was. It only mattered that they had a gun.

Brooklyn's voice crackled. His timbre was lost in static. "Target acquired," he said. "Target 001."

Rommond glanced at the shotgun on the floor, then to his holster, but knew he could not reach the revolver in time. He thought he could drop or dodge, but Brooklyn's gun was too close. Then he wondered if finally his time had come. He had escaped death before, probably more than his fair due. His debts were finally to be collected.

He closed his eyes, and heard that tiny click, the mechanical equivalent of a death knell.

The bullet felt like fire, a burn that pierced inside, branding him.

Brooklyn fell, dropping his own branding iron. The shot fired, entering the wall. When he hit the floor, Brooklyn saw what at first looked like a Regime soldier, but then looked like Taberah, her hair partly tied up and partly tumbling, her uniform unkempt, her gun still smoking.

Rommond turned. He already had his gun ready. The show was over. He did not want an encore.

Brooklyn moaned and squirmed upon the floor, clutching the wound.

"I didn't want to have to do this," Rommond said, shaking his head.

Brooklyn had no words, just murmurs of pain.

Taberah kept her gun pointed at Brooklyn, and kept her finger ready to twitch.

"Put that away," Rommond told her.

"You told me to keep an eye on him," she said. "That was my task, and that's what I'm doing."

"He's down," the general replied. "You can stand down too."

"You've got this?" she asked, with a hint of doubt. Then again, she always thought he did not have what it took to lead the Resistance. He never doubted her in that regard.

"I've got this," Rommond said, nodding slowly.

"Don't blame me if you die," she said. "I've enough ghosts haunting me."

She left the room, and for a moment it seemed like she stood outside, waiting to hear some attack, so that she could storm in and finish what she started, and get to say "I told you so." It never happened, and her silhouette passed on the next fight, the shape of her gun still raised, and her finger undoubtedly still itching on the trigger.

"Your first bullet," Rommond said, crouching down to Brooklyn. "I remember mine. Oh, I'm surprised I do. So many years ago. I've had quite a few since then."

That faded look passed from Brooklyn's eyes. Rommond could see the man again, as if an invisible armour had fallen off. He was unplugged again. It was just a pity that a bullet was needed to sever the wires.

Brooklyn looked like he wanted to talk, but could not, as if the machine in him prohibited it. Rommond wondered what he might have said. *It hurts*, he thought, remembering his own first branding. *It hurts like Hell.* He watched Brooklyn's laboured breaths. Taberah got him in the back, like she often did, but this time she did it on orders, the kind of orders that Rommond hated to give. *It knocks the breath out of you*, he thought. He just hoped it knocked the Regime out of Brooklyn too.

"Let's get you cleaned up," Rommond said.

"No," Brooklyn said with a sigh. "Just let me bleed."

Rommond's brow furrowed. "I would have taken that bullet in your gun. I would have taken it for you. Would you have let *me* bleed?"

Brooklyn could not hold his gaze. "I would have *made* you bleed. That is why I should bleed instead. Let me leave this world, Rommond. I do not belong here any more. I am not *me* any more."

Rommond did not stir. "I believed in you when you stood in Blackout among the Iron Guard. I knew then that deep beneath the wires, there were arteries that pumped blood—your blood. I believed in you then when I could barely see your face. Don't tell me to give up on you when I can see you more."

"You see a memory," Brooklyn said. "I see it too. But it is fading."

"It is stronger than it has ever been."

"You believe. I wish I could believe it too."

"Don't give up on me, Brooklyn. I won't give up on you. I gave up before when I thought you were dead, when I should *never* have given up. I should have stayed strong for you. I should never have trusted their words, their lies."

"You should have never trusted me," Brooklyn whimpered. "I told you I would betray you." He held up his hand, which, though it was metal, quivered before him. "This ... this is not *my* hand. This is theirs. They made it. They own it." He pointed to himself with his other hand. "They own me."

"They don't," Rommond said. "Their devices make up only a portion of you. The rest of you ... is still you." He tried to hold Brooklyn's hand, his real hand, his human hand, but Brooklyn took it away, as if the Regime had ordered him to.

"They own enough that it does not matter."

Rommond shook his head violently. "What about your mind? What about your soul?" He paused, then placed the palm of his hand on Brooklyn's chest. "What about ... your heart?" There was a waver in his voice, which he tried to bury.

Brooklyn looked at him this time, instead of away from him. There was resignation in his eyes, that same look that so many saw in Rommond when he thought Brooklyn was dead. It was the same look, because Brooklyn thought that he was dead too.

"Stay with me, Brooklyn, please," Rommond begged. "I can't lose you again. I'm not sure there's enough of my heart left to break."

It was not the voice of a general, a commander, a superior. It was the voice of a partner, a lover, a confidante. It was not so certain. It was not so stern.

"How can I stay?" Brooklyn asked. "I do not know who I am any more."

"You're Kia-ooba-lukassa," Rommond said softly. "You're Brooklyn."

Taberah came back in. It seemed she had not gone far, and was listening at the door.

"You're not alone, Brooklyn," she said. "I lost myself, and I'm not sure I've found me again. Sometimes things just stay lost. And sometimes you just need to search harder."

Brooklyn shook his head. "I do not know where to look. I feel I am in prison. Why search if I can only search my cell?"

"Then let's find your jailer first," Taberah said. "Let's set you free."

Chapter Thirty-three

ALMA MATER

Alakovi saw the Conductor as it fell to the ground, and she also saw it get back up just as quickly. She knew that Lokk could get Rommond where he needed to be, but not if that mechanical beast was chasing them. It had to be stopped or slowed. That was her task.

She pressed the horn on her bike, sounding the alarm, issuing the biker battle cry. The other Copper Vixens turned and rallied to her, abandoning whatever they were doing. There was the sound of revving engines, and the sight of steam, and the smell of oil. All of the Vixens converged on the Conductor, with the Copper Matron leading the charge.

She fired from her shotgun as she approached, but the bullets bounced off the metal plating. The force of the blast pushed it back, but it only stalled it. It was not her idea of a solution, but stalling would have to do. The bikes circled around it, creating a whirlwind of dust, as if they too could summon dust devils to mask their travel. The Vixens pummelled the machine creature with bullets, some of which almost struck their own on the other side. But still the Conductor stepped forward, ignoring the iron and the sand.

It seized one of the Vixens as it approached, tearing her from her bike, knocking the other one off, and letting the bike spin off and topple over. The woman screamed and kicked as the metal gauntlet closed around her throat, muffling her screams and weakening her kicks.

The sound was like an alarm of its own to the Copper Matron, who stopped her bike and turned once against to the Conductor, casting aside her shotgun, placing both hands firmly upon the handlebars. Instead of a bullet, she fired her bike at the beast, driving straight into it as fast as she could. It tumbled, and she tumbled, and the dead Vixen tumbled from its hand. She rolled in the sand for a moment, but as she rolled she saw the lifeless face of one of her own. She clambered up, letting out a terrible roar, and she raced over to the Conductor, which was now attempting to climb up the side of the Landquaker. She seized it with her strong hands, hands cracked and weathered, conditioned by harsh life, hands that might as well have been iron. She dragged that ton of metal limbs from the railway gun and flung it through the air. As soon as it landed, it began to straighten up again.

The Vixens circled it once more, but this time the Conductor grabbed two of them and held them up by the shoulders, before driving their heads together with such force that it crushed their skulls. The bellow Alakovi let out then was like the combined cry of every mother who witnessed the death of their child at the hands of an attacker. It was a wild cry, and the

Copper Matron felt the wilderness welling up inside her, struggling to get free.

She charged, her feet cracking the parched earth beneath her, her boots leaving little graveyards in the sand. Despite her size and stature, she moved like lightning, and she growled like thunder, and when she struck the Conductor, her grasping claws outreached, she hit like a tidal wave. It fell, and she fell upon it like a hammer. If it was an anvil, it was about to be crushed.

She punched it with her fists, striking metal and wire and tubing. It struggled with her, grasping her arms and kicking her from it. Then it restored its eyes on Rommond on the roof. He was the priority. He was Target 001.

It marched back to the halted Landquaker, and began to climb again, creating climbing hooks by punching the tips of its fingers through the chassis. Yet as it climbed, Alakovi came upon it once more, tearing it down, leaving the markings of its claws in the hull. It tried another time, but she pulled it down, and another, but she took and it held it to the ground this time.

The force with which she punched its face, or whatever it was it had for a face, broke her own fingers and knuckles, and left huge dents in the metal. Sparks spat from the wounds, as if to solder up her own. She yelled through the stabbing pain, using that pain to stab back with her buckled hand.

But the Conductor did not feel pain, and it had no empathy to feel hers either. It had nothing but its mission, which made it more deadly than a human or a demon. It grabbed her right arm and snapped it. She cried out, and the Vixens heard her cry, and the Conductor heard it, but it was completely unmoved by it. While the Iron Wall fenced off the Regime territory, the Conductor was its own kind of wall, falling upon and crushing people, feeling nothing but their bodies beneath its iron bricks.

She wrapped her left arm around its right one and tugged it from its socket, pulling out wires, freeing the tiny sparks from the prison of its body. It did not cry out, but she continued to bash it, as if somehow deep inside her she thought she might find a part of it that could feel pain. She had already made a vow that it would. Now she was just fulfilling it.

Yet it only needed one arm to throw her from it. She landed upon one of the fallen bikes. From there she could see several of the Vixens driving their own hogs into the Conductor, keeping it from the Landquaker, keeping it from its mission. In that moment she thought that perhaps that was pain to it, being unable to fulfil its sole task. But she wanted something more, something tangible.

She grabbed a broken metal bar from the bike and launched herself at the Conductor again, whacking it across the head, hearing the awful clatter of crashing metal, and feeling the vibration rising into her one good arm like the aftershock of an earthquake. Again she pounded it, adding dints inside the dints, making it look more like the monster that it really was.

Her fingers bled. The broken bones shattered even more, but still she bashed the creature with the splinters. With her other hand she clawed at wires behind the Conductor's head, tearing out everything she could. The fires in its eyes weakened, but they did not fully go out.

Its right hand twitched, but did not reach to strangle her, but its left hand still had all its strength. It reached for her face, seizing her by the nose and chin. It clasped so tightly that she felt her jaw shatter, and her nose broke in place. She screamed out and shook its claw from her, before it kicked her once again into the sand.

It rose up, but now its walk was disjointed. Its right arm hung from its tendons made of wires, and oil leaked out from it like blood. It clutched the side of the Landquaker, even as it started to shift, but Alakovi was there again, clutching it in turn. She head-butted the back of its head with such force that its face went through the hull of the train. It struggled to dislodge itself, and the railway gun pulled it along slowly as its wheels ramped up. Alakovi was dragged with it, and she struggled to break through its own hull, reaching in to the delicate wiring beneath.

The man in it must have noticed, for its survival instincts kicked in. Its working arm swivelled in place until it grabbed the Copper Matron by the throat. It squeezed, even as she squeezed her own working hand into a crevice in the Conductor's torso. She started to choke. She felt the suffocation, the starvation of oxygen, and the crushing force of the Iron Guard's gauntlet. She felt the blood on her forehead dripping into her eyes. She felt the pain in her hand and arm, and the pain throughout her body. She felt the life leaving her.

But she also felt anger for her fallen daughters, for her killed comrades. She felt a conviction stronger than anything she had felt before: that she would be this metal monster's own conductor, leading it to the gates of Hell. She ripped out whatever wires she could grab, and the creature's grip weakened, and it stuttered in place. Its joints no longer seemed like they could hold anything, and it collapsed upon itself, pulling Alakovi with it to the ground. She struggled from its lessened grip, bruised, bloodied, and broken.

But the fires burned anew in its eyes, and it once more tried to reach the Landquaker, but now it had to drag itself along the dust. She saw it move, and she crawled after it with one arm, hauling her broken body behind her. Everything was a struggle. Everything caused her pain, moving or staying still. Even her cries hurt. Her lungs ached as she breathed in and out air and sand.

She reached the Conductor's body and crawled on top of it. It continued to twitch and jerk, and the fires in its eyes kept reigniting. She would not stop until they went fully out. She tore at it with what little strength she had left in her. She forced her hand through a gap she had made in the plating. It was small, too small for her bulging muscles, and the metal sliced through her arm as she forced it inside. She felt around, until she felt a heart. She was not sure if it was a human or demon heart, and no one would ever know for sure, because she burst it between her fingers and ripped it from its place. The flames in the Conductor's eyes finally flickered out, and Alakovi rolled off it onto her back, feeling her own fires flickering.

Fighting raged on around her, but she could no longer move. She heard the cries of Copper Vixens, and her lips trembled as she realised she could do nothing to save them. All she could do was lie there and listen, and hear all the sounds as they faded out. It seemed like a long time passed, a lifetime. It was her life, and she watched it swiftly pass her by.

Then she saw Lokk's face, and she heard the humming of his engine. It was a reassuring sound. She hoped that it was a sound that existed in Heaven. She hoped she had earned her place there. Surely fighting demons was enough.

Lokk placed his hand behind her neck. He did not move her. She knew there was nothing that could be moved, nothing that was not broken. The only part of her that remained unscathed was her soul.

"We came to fight," she said, spluttering blood.

"Not to die," Lokk replied.

She forced a smile. "That's the ... biggest fight, isn't it?" The words were a struggle, a fight of their own.

"You've gotta win that one for me," Lokk said.

The Copper Matron's smile faded. It took too much strength to keep it in place. "Can't win them all," she said, her voice fading into a whisper.

Lokk held her less broken hand tightly. "You've earned your place with the Great Ox."

"I just hope," she said, "I earned back ... his trust."

"Who's trust?"

"Rommond."

"I don't think there was ever anything to earn back."

She nodded to herself solemnly. "There was. It shouldn't have been, but there was."

"What about the Vixens? Who will lead them now?"

She coughed and choked on her final words. "There'll always be … a Copper Matron."

What she said was true, for there were rules among that sorority for someone else to take her place, but they were untried and untested, and though someone new and younger might soon take that title, they would always think of Alakovi when they heard that name.

Chapter Thirty-four

THE CONTROLLER

The Landquaker was starting to pick up speed. Rommond and Taberah finally burned through the door to the control room, firing several shots at the crew inside. But the driver seat was taken by someone who was a little bit more than just the common crew.

It was her, the Controller. She had a name, but the Regime never used it. She had a role, and that became everything that mattered. That became her personality, her work, her rest, her life. She answered to no one but the Iron Emperor himself, for he was her controller, and yet it seemed that she did not even notice that, in her own way, she was just as much a machine as those beneath her.

She wore black armour, edged with silver, covering every part of her, leaving nothing exposed, not even her face, which was encased in a mask of many pieces, kept together with black fabric. When she talked, the pieces moved, almost like a puzzle, though the real puzzle was finding out who it was beneath the veil. Even her hair, if she had any, was hidden behind a plate of iron. Her hands were the same, covered in armour and cloth, never hindering her movement.

Upon her belt were many devices, all of which had many buttons. Some had aerials, some had cogs, and some had dials and metres. At the back of her belt were many canisters, containing a variety of gases and chemicals, and next to those were an array of tools, for she did not just control; she made and she repaired. To the Iron Guard, she was all. She was their mother, their maker, their god. They were programmed to bow down to her.

Rommond fired a shot at her, but the bullet bounced off her armour, and came back at him so fast that he barely had time to move out of the way.

She pressed a button and turned a dial upon her wrist, and Brooklyn's eyes flickered. He stood up sharply and grabbed Rommond by the shoulders, pushing him against the wall. The general struggled, but the grip was tight.

Taberah charged into the control room, launching herself at the Controller, tackling her to the ground, knocking a canister from her hand. They struggled on the floor, until Taberah dragged the Controller up, bashing her against the counter.

"You can't control me," Taberah said, grasping for the woman's throat. She could see her eyes through the mask, the only part of her that was visible, and despite all that was said about them being the window to the soul, Taberah could see nothing in them, as if they too were masked, or if she did not have a soul.

"We are all machines," the Controller replied. "We do not act. We react. We're all programmed by something. Call it nature. Call it God." She scoffed at the latter. "Call it me."

Taberah cocked her head. "Well. React to this." She smashed the Controller's head against the controls. A piece of her mask tumbled to the floor, and her skin was burnt and blackened beneath. She coiled over, hiding her face. "The pain … is just a symptom."

"Well, whatever you've got," Taberah said, "I'm the cure."

She struck again, knocking the Controller down to her knees.

"How arrogant you are," the Controller said. "Did you not think that maybe I just wanted you to let me fall?" She reached for the fallen canister, and before Taberah could get to her, she pulled the pin. A green gas sprayed out, and in the haze it seemed that the Controller simply disappeared.

Taberah ran from the room, to where Rommond was slowly overpowering Brooklyn, and Brooklyn was slowly coming to himself again.

"We need gas masks!" she cried to Rommond.

"They're in the control room," Rommond said, still struggling. "Under the counter."

Taberah dived back into the smoke, reaching around until she found a box of gas masks. She grabbed one for herself, inhaling hard, and dragged the rest outside. Rommond shoved one in Brooklyn's face, before putting on his own. Taberah crouched on the ground, gasping oxygen.

Rommond walked into the haze, holding his gas mask up against his mouth.

Taberah stood up and looked around. From

the window in one of the doors, she could see the Controller racing down the corridor towards the rear of the railway gun. She moved to chase her, but Brooklyn held her back.

"Let her go," he said. "We have mission here. We need to stop Landquaker."

"Everyone has a mission," Taberah replied, and she pointed to the fleeing Controller. "I think that's yours."

"Damn it!" Rommond shouted, emerging from the haze. "She's broken the controls." He held up the snapped lever.

"We can't stop it?" Brooklyn asked.

"Well, Rommond," Taberah said, her voice muffled by the gas mask. "I think you better play that Ace you've been saving."

Chapter Thirty-five

RAIN OF THE RAILS

Jacob, Whistler and Lorelai eventually found their way to the control room, where the gas had dissipated. The nurse started to tend to Brooklyn's gunshot wound, while Rommond and Taberah rooted through boxes, the general periodically looking up to fire a shot at a passing Regime soldier.

"What are we looking for?" Jacob asked.

"A radio," Rommond replied.

Jacob thought it was probably best if he did not tell him what he had done with the last one he encountered.

He and Whistler joined the rummaging, falling over every now and then as the train hurtled along even faster than before. After much fruitless searching, the boy eventually found a two-way radio among the Regime supplies.

"Got one!" he cried.

Rommond grabbed it. There was no *please* or *thank you*. There was no time for it. The general fiddled with the knob, trying to tune in to a designated channel. He knew there would be Regime forces listening. They were always listening. Yet he knew by now he had more than announced where he was, and what he was up to. *Still*, he thought, *I might surprise them*.

"Desert Hawk here," he said.

"Rainmaker," someone replied on the other end, his voice crackling.

"We need rain," the general said. "Over and out."

Who knew what the Regime made of this brief exchange, but Rommond knew it would worry them. He *liked* that it would worry them. He just hoped the card he had tucked up his sleeve for so long was still there for him to play. It was Plan B. He did not have another one.

"We better buckle up," he said.

"Can't we just get off?" Whistler asked.

"At this speed," Rommond said, "if you jump, you might as well jump to Heaven."

They found seats wherever they could, and tied their belts up tight. Jacob and Whistler sat in one room. Rommond, Taberah and Brooklyn sat in the next, and Lorelai sat on her own further on. Then they stared outside the windows, following Rommond's lead, and they stared for a long time, until they thought they saw something in the distance. They looked some more, until it was clear what they were seeing.

The sky lit up with the bright colours of the Treasury's fleet of hot air balloons, which had lost their Regime-sponsored crew, replaced by more amenable men appointed by the Baroness Ebronah. The aerial advance was led by the Skyshaker, piloted by Cantro, who had lost nothing of his acrobatic skills.

An alarm went off in the Landquaker, the kind of dull, groaning alarm that rose and fell, the warning of a bombing raid.

Several Regime crewmen charged through where the Resistance members sat strapped up. Most of them paid them no heed, focusing on their urgent duties, but one of them stopped and looked at the general, bemused.

"We're fine for tea, thank you," Rommond said, unloading a bullet from his gun.

"Hell," Jacob shouted over. He could hear the body slumping. "I could do with a whiskey instead."

The crew of the Landquaker immediately hoisted the gun up, one slow latch at a time, each notch clicking into place like the sound of a gigantic clock, counting down the seconds till the Treasury's coffers would be scattered in the sand.

Cantro propelled the Skyshaker ahead of the Treasury fleet. Unlike them, he did not need to rely on the good will of the wind. The airship made its own wind, zooming through the sky in crusader mode, even as an army of the air marched behind to join the crusade.

The railway gun locked into place, and it too zoomed, speeding down the tracks on a mission of its own. The Regime fired a shell at the Skyshaker, which Cantro easily dodged, and as he flew back over the tracks ahead of the Landquaker, he dropped a bomb, which tore a hole in the train's path.

Yet despite this, the Landquaker's speed was so great that it sailed over the missing track, barely rocking any more than normal. Its many wheels, held together in a frame, span ferociously, grinding against the iron rails, keeping its gigantic hull firmly in place.

Cantro turned and passed over again, but before he could drop another bomb, the Landquaker let loose its own, firing a canister into the air that was unlike any of the shells it had previously used. The skypilot evaded it again, but it did not need a direct impact. It exploded nearby, sending nails and shrapnel in all directions, many of which bounced off the hull of the Skyshaker, and some of which pierced the envelope encasing its balloons.

Cantro lost some control and was forced to retreat, the vessel sinking a little as he fled. It was not a good sight for the Resistance aboard the Landquaker, and it instilled new courage and conviction in the Regime forces there, who knew they just had to wait it out long enough to reach the well-defended docking bay fortress at the harbour further south.

It was then the turn of the Treasury. Ebronah kept a handful of the same crew, the more seasoned pilots who had sworn an oath to profit instead of the Regime. They had faced the Skyshaker in battle, so it was an odd feeling to be following it into a war against their former ally. For some, it was a welcome change, for they still felt their old allegiances. For others, seeing Cantro forced to retreat gave them a little hint of joy. It would not last, because with the Skyshaker out of the picture, all that was left was the Treasury's many colours, and the Regime's intent to paint them all red.

The Landquaker fired another canister, which

ripped through the weaker balloons of the Treasury fleet, sending some careering down, some plummeting, and some torn completely to shreds. Amidst the explosions and the cries, the Treasury dropped its own payload, bombs that were smaller than the ones aboard the Skyshaker, but ones that, in numbers, could rip apart those tracks. Numbers were the Treasury's only advantage, having spent so long counting gold and iron.

The tracks shuddered under the force of the blasts, but Jacob had worked on that railway as a child, back when the tracks were laid for transport, not for war. He knew that they were designed to take a beating, and they had since been enhanced by Brooklyn for the heavier frame of the Landquaker. The Iron Wall would not fall so easily. Many of the tracks held, and those that did not were merely cracked or weakened. More bombs fell, and the Treasury's fleet seemed endless, and its bomb supply unlimited, but the tracks themselves seemed to go on forever, like a ladder up to Heaven, or a stairway down to Hell.

Then Cantro re-emerged from the clouds, having forced the Skyshaker up as high as it could go. He did not have time to repair the envelope, and so little crew to do the repairs, so all he could do was expend steam, giving it a momentary lift, and let it sink slowly from its camouflage in the clouds, pushing it on with its tail-fin, propelling it that little bit faster than the Landquaker. As it descended, Cantro released its bombs in lots, three at a time, rocking the rails below, tearing the beams up, breaking and bending the metal. Yet the railway gun still chugged on. Cantro managed to keep just ahead of the train's gun, but he was dropping fast, and the Landquaker's barrel was still aimed high.

Then the wind betrayed him, blowing against the Skyshaker, as if something had dropped bombs on the airship's own tracks. He was losing speed fast, and the Landquaker was catching up. He released the last of his payload, which tore through the tracks and almost toppled the railway gun, tearing through the cowcatcher at the front, but still it was not enough to take it down. So Cantro did what he knew Rommond would do; he dipped the nose of the airship and made it dive even faster, right towards the tracks. The Landquaker's canisters of exploding nails helped in its descent, freeing more of the air in the balloons. Then it crashed before the Landquaker, and the train drove straight into it and up onto it, catching the airship beneath its wheels. It skidded on, sending sparks everywhere, until it veered off the tracks entirely and turned upon its side. There it slid through the desert for a time, throwing people around inside, and throwing the sand outside high into the air.

Cantro and his skeleton crew had left the Skyshaker just in time, parachuting down and landing behind the toppled gate of the Iron Wall. Smoke and sand rose for a time, and it dissipated slowly, revealing the crippled ruins of the railway gun. Rommond had hoped to keep the train intact, to restore it as a roving bastion of the Resistance. That plan had failed, but the backup plan worked. *If you cannot take the Wall, then break it.* The only question was: had Rommond's team survived beneath the fallen bricks?

Chapter Thirty-six

THE CARRIAGE SMOG

Inside the Landquaker, Jacob could barely see a thing. All the oil lamps were shattered, and some of them had started fires, adding more smoke to the haze. He heard people coughing, and felt hands reaching out for him.

He tore open his belt and stumbled out of the seat. He heard glass crushing beneath his boots. He knew he was standing on a window pane, and the Landquaker was on its side. He advanced slowly, reaching out in front of him.

"Whistler!" he cried out, choking on the fumes. "Taberah!"

He reached where he remembered Whistler had buckled up, and found the boy struggling to free himself, a task exacerbated by his mounting panic. Jacob had to feel about on the floor for a piece of the shattered window pane, which he used to cut Whistler loose.

"Meet outside," he heard Rommond call from the other room, followed by a chesty cough. "Don't stay in here."

The problem was finding a way out.

Jacob felt something smack his head, and he

reached down to find a gas mask there. Someone, probably Rommond or Taberah, was throwing them out in all directions. It might even have been Regime soldiers. Jacob could not find another in the smoke, so he handed it to Whistler, who held it to his face. Jacob pushed the boy onwards, towards where he thought he saw a little light through the black smoke. He held his arm up to his mouth, coughing into his uniform.

It was light all right, but it was the light of a fire, not the sun, so they were forced to retreat again. They might have stood on a body, but they did not stay long enough to find out. Jacob just hoped it was not one of his companions.

They scrambled through a hole in the wall leading to the next room, but they could not find a way to get into the corridor, which was now above them instead of beside them. They reached around, trying to find more openings, but it seemed like they were trapped there.

"I can't see," Whistler cried.

"Just hold on," Jacob replied, grabbing him by the arm. He reached around until he felt what seemed like a chair, and dragged it over to what was once the floor of the Landquaker, but now was the wall. It was difficult to adjust to all the shifting pieces. The world had turned on its side, but their minds had not turned with it.

"We're going to have to climb," the smuggler said.

"I'm no good at climbing," Whistler replied.

Jacob felt around in the haze with one hand, still clutching Whistler's arm with the other. His feet struck what he thought might be a chest of drawers, which had fallen over. Or maybe it was the right way up. The floor had fallen over instead.

"You'll have to help me lift this up," he said, spluttering as the dust invaded his lungs.

Whistler reached down. "I don't know what I'm looking for," he said.

"It's a cabinet. Just grab the edge. I'll grab the other side."

Jacob might as well have told Whistler to stand back, because the boy was little use in hauling the chest of drawers up. He had barely any strength, and he squirmed and yelped as two of the drawers fell out. It was a struggle for Jacob to haul it up, but he managed to get it standing, and pushed it over towards the chair.

"Okay, kid, I need you to climb this," he said. He dragged the boy over, aware that at any moment he might breathe in too much smoke and pass out. The smog was already getting to him, and his head was just as clouded. Time was against them. It always was.

"I don't think I can," Whistler said, his voice a little muffled by the gas mask.

"Trust me, kid, you can. I'll help you. Put your hand here." He guided Whistler's hands towards the chair. "Climb up on that." He hauled him up as much as the boy climbed, then guided Whistler's hands to the cabinet. "Grab onto that." He pushed him up again.

"What about you?" Whistler called back.

"Don't you worry about me," Jacob said. "I'll be fine." He did not feel as confident as he tried to sound.

He clambered up the makeshift stairs, joining Whistler at the top, emerging into what was once the corridor, and now was more of a dusty attic. It was just as dark there, and the smog was spreading. The periodic fires were no help; they spat out a thick black smoke, which roamed the vessel, seeking to smother everything.

"We're going to have to walk across here," Jacob said. They were standing on what was previously the wall of one of the rooms. They just had to be careful not to stand on a door that opened inwards, or they would fall back down again.

"How are we going to get out?" Whistler pleaded.

"We'll make it, kid. We'll make it." It was the same promise he made to Whistler in the desert several months earlier, and it was a promise he desperately wanted to keep.

He took a fit of coughing. The smoke was getting to him.

"Take my mask, Jacob," Whistler offered.

"No, I—"

"Take it!"

He felt the mask being shoved into his hand. He held it to his mouth for a moment, just enough to catch his breath, then handed it back to the boy.

"I need you to wear that," he said. "Please, kid."

They saw light streaming in from one of the rooms above them up ahead, but there was a gap between the two walls that they were using as floors. It was not clear if it was an open door that formed the gap, or if it was a hole. All that mattered is that it formed a chasm. They were not even entirely sure there was another side to land on, but Jacob threw a piece of broken timber over, and the sound seemed like maybe there was.

"We have to jump," he said.

Whistler was growing more panicked by the second. "I can't see where we're jumping."

"Put your foot out and feel the edge."

"What if I don't make it?"

"You'll make it, kid," he panted. He just was not so sure about himself.

They leapt across, thankful that there was indeed somewhere to leap across to. The light was so much closer now. In time they were in it, and they could see more clearly, but even there the smoke was thick. Whistler's worry must have doubled then, because he could see how faint Jacob was. He clutched his arm tighter, as if somehow he could help pump the blood.

Jacob knew he had to hold out a little longer. He had to get Whistler out alive.

It was at this point that Whistler's bravery kicked in, and he started reaching around for things to climb up on. He found the broken door, but struggled to move it.

"We can make a ramp!" he said.

Jacob helped haul it into place, but everything was that much more of a struggle. He felt he had no energy left to give. Not enough to live.

"Come on!" Whistler shouted, pushing Jacob up the ramp, slipping as they went. They found themselves in the next room, which had now become the third floor, and the light was stronger now. They could just about see daylight outside, and it was blinding.

Jacob helped Whistler up onto a fallen box, ignoring the pain of the splinters, but it did not seem like there was much else there for them to climb upon. The smashed window up above, which was now a skylight, was still a little out of reach.

"You have to … get up … on my shoulders," Jacob said.

"I'm not leaving you."

"You can pull me up after." Jacob knew Whistler would not be able to. It did not matter. He just had to get the boy outside. That was all that mattered now.

Whistler reluctantly agreed, and Jacob hoisted him up. Despite Whistler's small stature, it was not easy to do. The strength was sapped from him.

"I still can't reach!" Whistler cried, his fingers barely touching the remaining shards of glass.

There was a shimmer of white linen, and Whistler heard Lorelai's voice. "Grab my hand," she said. He reached up, and she grabbed his wrist, but he heard a thud behind him as Jacob collapsed to the floor, his arm dangling over the drop to the lower level.

"No!" Whistler cried. "No, let me go. I have to save Jacob!"

"I'll get him," Tardo said, appearing at the window as Lorelai dragged Whistler out.

The *maran* soldier lowered himself back into the carriage on a makeshift rope, and dragged Jacob outside. Whistler saw people emerging from windows further up on either side, and one of them was Rommond, hauling Brooklyn on his back. Taberah was outside, helping to pull them out.

They all gathered outside and away from the crash site, where Cantro had set up cover from the sun and the sand with his tattered parachute.

There were few Regime survivors. Some fled, while others surrendered, knowing that the journey to a Regime-held stronghold was far, and the unforgiving sun was chasing them. Treasury balloons began to land around the smoulder of the Landquaker, bringing water and medical supplies to the Resistance survivors, and pointed guns to the Regime.

"Hell," Jacob said, coughing as he came to, finding Whistler bathing his forehead with a damp cloth. "Remind me to never ride a train again."

Chapter Thirty-seven

AWAKENING

They surveyed the carcass of the Landquaker. The gun was broken off the top, lying half submerged in sand. There were small fires throughout the vehicle, and the damage was extensive. There was not a window that had not shattered, and everyone, living and dead, had the cuts to prove it.

"This isn't exactly what I wanted," the general said. "I had hoped we could salvage it, take it back for our own use. You can breach the enemy's castle, or you can take it and use it yourself." He shook his head solemnly. "We could have used this to take the port in the south."

"Well, it's better broken than in their hands," Taberah said.

Brooklyn returned from his extensive rummaging through the ruins.

"Can you fix it?" Rommond asked.

"I do not think I can, Rommond. I think I need to fix myself first."

"We'll have to leave it here," Jacob said. "Unless there's something you can salvage."

"You can't just leave that here," Tardo objected.

"He's right," Lokk said, still perched upon his bike.

"If the Regime doesn't come for it, the Clockwork Commune will."

"Those scavengers will never get this," Rommond promised. "We'll haul it back to Blackout, brick by brick if we have to. Will the Oxen join us?"

"No," Lokk replied, nodding towards the wrapped body on the back of his bike. "I have my own affairs to attend to. I can't bury her out here. I can't let the scavengers pick her bones."

Rommond nodded solemnly. "It is a great loss."

"Greater than you know."

The Oxen departed, letting their black leather mingle with the night. The surviving Copper Vixens, of which there were only five, joined them, needing to see their Matron through to the final end. Whether or not they would return to the Resistance, Rommond did not know. What he did know was that without Alakovi, they would just not be the same.

The Resistance forces rested at the scene that night, regrouping with some of the tribespeople, who had, with Leadman's help, secured Fort Landlock in the north. The next day was spent throwing ropes around the giant gun, and tying them to whatever was left of Leadman's platoon. He wanted to leave it behind, but Rommond was the one calling the shots. He had a big enough gun to call them, even if the barrel was broken.

They drove back to Blackout slowly, and many walked, because there were not enough vehicles for them all. They passed by the mangled remains of many landships lost in the recent battle, and found the Long Spyglass, which Rommond made sure they added to their train.

They journeyed for hours, resting little. They sat in the sun, hiding beneath their hats, but Brooklyn was the only one who did not keep his eyes to the sand. He stared with a worried look into the sky.

"What is it?" Rommond asked him.

Jacob looked up and saw a speck hurtling through the air. *A bird*, he thought, but it did not fly like a bird, and it seemed too far up. He felt his heart beat, like those flapping wings might beat against the wind. Something felt very wrong.

People began to gather. Eyes turned like turrets to the sky, as if they could shoot down whatever it was that flew there. What ammunition they had in those nervous glares fired like blanks, until all they were left with was the empty shells in their hearts.

"We need to repair that airship!" Taberah shouted, but Cantro did not seem confident that the Skyshaker could even be repaired.

"No," Rommond said. "We don't know what it is yet." He whispered this last part, as if it might have incredible hearing, as if it might be some kind of demon, some kind of monster with wicked wings.

Jacob strained his eyes, but the more he strained them, the less it seemed he needed to. Whatever it was, it was coming closer. It was dropping fast. There was now a trail of smoke behind that phantom figure, as if its feet or talons burned, like they might if it had come from Hell.

There was alarm in every face, ringing out from the bell-tower of their eyes. Some of Rommond's lieutenants looked to one another as if they knew exactly what that creature was. They did not look to the general—they feared that he might confirm their terror.

Rommond was already racing towards the Long Spyglass, trying to see while others were starting to turn their eyes away, and looking for places to hide. The open expanse of the desert offered little refuge. Jacob was closest to Brooklyn's gigantic scope, and though the fear of others infected him, his curiosity was the cure.

He reached the Long Spyglass and placed his eye to the lens. All he saw was cloud, so he had to reposition it several times. Then he saw it, clear as day, as if the clouds no longer tried to hide it, as if they had revealed the conspiracy of the sky.

It was a contraption of the air. A wooden frame with wings and a propeller. Like one of those in Brooklyn's designs. They said they could not get them to fly for long. They said they could not get them to reach great heights. They said that these so-called "aeroplanes" would not change the war. They were wrong.

It was painted a gaudy yellow. Whoever flew it, whoever was mad enough to risk their life in that rickety vessel, did not want to hide. They wanted to be noticed. They wanted to be seen.

Rommond reached the spyglass, panting. He placed a heavy hand upon its frame. "What do you see?" he asked.

But Jacob's eyes were seized by another sight. It was not the plane that held his gaze. It was what the plane was carrying. Ropes strung down from every part of the flying machine, tied to a bulbous iron casing below. A bomb. A giant bomb.

Jacob could not help but remember Rommond's fateful words: "I think the war of the air is over." *No*, he thought, *it's just begun.*

"What is it?" Rommond barked, pushing Jacob aside and casting his eagle eye upon the lens.

People began shouting over, as if they had seen it too, but they could not see it with their naked eyes. They merely felt it in their thumping hearts. Taberah charged up, panting the words: "It's spelling something in the sky, in the smoke."

Jacob looked up. He could see it too.

It read: *The world will wake.*

The letters were large. The fear they evoked was even larger.

Rommond stumbled as he took his eye away from the spyglass. He looked at Taberah with apologetic eyes. He did not seek out Brooklyn in the crowd, for to him he felt an apology would seem weak. And to the world, no apology was enough.

"They did it," he said, faltering and shaking his head. "They ... no."

"Who?" Taberah asked. "What did they do?"

"The Armageddon Brigade," he said, and then he gestured to himself. "I created a monster."

Jacob looked into the spyglass again, hoping what he had seen was wrong, hoping his eyes had betrayed him. Yet the only betrayal was that colossal bomb, that tool of destruction that he had seen unfinished beneath the hidden floor of Rommond's submarine, which he thought was locked safely in the vault of the abyss. But it was finished now, and it was not safely tucked away. It was there in the sky, for all to see, and it would be there on the ground, for all to feel, until there was no such thing as feeling. The smoke spewed from a flume upon the plane's back, but through the smog the bomb seemed to swim. On either side of its metal hull was blazoned the eyes and teeth of a shark, and on the bottom was painted the last words that the living might read before they roused from the dream of life: Worldwaker.

ABOUT THE AUTHOR

Dean F. Wilson was born in Dublin, Ireland in 1987. He started writing at age 11, when he began his first (unpublished) novel, entitled *The Power Source*. He won a TAP Educational Award from Trinity College Dublin for an early draft of *The Call of Agon* (then called *Protos Mythos*) in 2001.

He is the author of the *Children of Telm* epic fantasy trilogy and the *Great Iron War* steampunk series.

Dean also works as a journalist, primarily in the field of technology. He has written for *TechEye*, *Thinq*, *V3*, *VR-Zone*, *ITProPortal*, *TechRadar Pro*, and *The Inquirer*.

www.deanfwilson.com